12 Speed

Ryan S. Lewis

12 Speed

First Edition: 2022

ISBN: 9781524316679
ISBN eBook: 9781524316822

© of the text:
  Ryan S. Lewis

© Layout, design and production of this edition: 2022 EBL Books

*This book is dedicated and created in the
conscious memory of a hero of social troubles...*

*In loving memory of John Shick. That who committed
suicide by committing a shooting spree at the place...*

12 SPEED...
RIDE INTUIT...

The WARD'd

Brian is sitting on the bed in the empty room as a lady walks in. She has a name tag and a clipboard.

"Brian?" She asks, "Are you Brian?"

"Yes" He responded looking up from a blank stare at the wall. "Are you here to tell me I can leave?" He asks and laughs "Maybe we are having some.. leaving issues?" Brian laughs.. as he points to the wall.. "looks like an off white peach, but not pink.. Fancy.."

The nurse squints across the room and pauses. "No, I don't think.. You can leave when the doctors say so...um I'm here to..." She pauses again.

"Oh.. You don't think?" Brian questions and laughs again..

"Would you like to talk to me for a minute?" -She asks slowly..

"Do I really have a choice?" -Brian asks

"Well, Brian if you don't want to talk with me now I'll have to keep a note of that and come back another time. It says you haven't been taking any medication that the doctors prescribe." -Nurse

"I don't know what the hell type of medications ya'll think you want to play with but .. I'm fine.. Or maybe something.. is wrong with me.. I keep having this ringing problem in my ears.. regardless of what I think or whatnot .. and my neck hurts.. or something.." -Brian

"Have you been hearing voices or anything?" - The nurse asks as she motions with some paperwork..

"Hearing voices?" -Brian leans back a bit.. "Is there some reason why I'm not supposed to be hearing voices?"

The nurse looks up "Excuse me?"

Brian thinks.. "Is there some reason I shouldn't be able to hear people's voices?"

The nurse answers - "oh no.. I meant ..voices that aren't there.."

Brian laughs into a coughing cluster of hacks and acts dramatic.. "Can I hear people that aren't supposed to be here?.. What the fuck? Are you saying that .. I'm not supposed to be here? Or.. I'm not supposed to be able to hear what you asked me? Because if this is some type of riddle of sexual prowess.. I think I need to be able to hear voices.." -Brian

The nurse stands to cross the room towards the door while scratching a note..

"No, you must've been... doing something.." The nurse says strangely and squinting and sits on the empty bed across from him.

"It was just anxiety... I think.." He says while taking in a big breath "I think it was.. I mean, I'm pretty sure it was.. like a panic attack."

"When did this happen?" She asked Brian and scratched at notes as if he was third eye blind or something..

Brian Responds - "Somewhere between my death making more sense than my life combined with an empty hope for success.."

"Well, that's what I want to talk about with you then.. Why do you think that happened?" - The nurse claims..

"Well... I keep getting this weird dream.." -Brian

The Hallway

"Brian.. Brian, Hello .. You there?"

She stands over him as he looks up confused and she looks back snickering..

"Well, what happened? Looks like you got a cut on your head.." -she said

Brian looks around from the ground and rugs up to a staggering stunt of remembering what..

Wrinkling his nose into the setting sunshine as he points at the streetlamp on the sidewalk. "No, um.. Oh Yeah, I must've run into this light-post." -he claims while reaching up and feeling the cut on his head...

The young girl responded with a bright laughter that snickered into a kackling at hymn like a green day that was stoned for the temple of pilots..

"I was trying to tie my shoe and I swerved and didn't see it.. I think.. Or did I?" -Brian Contended and rubbing his head..

"You were trying to tie your shoe while the bike was moving?" She asks "And where'd this bike come from?" ..

"What does it matter? I don't know. I just found it or something.." Brian throws his hands up in the air and falls back into the grass next to the park he was riding out from.. "Sheeeesh, it got caught on the chain guard or something.."

"Did you steal it?" -She insists in question..

"What?" -He raps back at the girl.. "What the hell does it matter to you? Where the heck were you going to?"

"I was just walking to the band music thang at the park.." And then I saw you on the ground.." She responds mudhoney'd as it gets..

Brian gets back up and grabs up the bike .. "Maybe, I stole it.. But, I think it really needed some real love at any rate of coincidence." He persists as he picks the bike up into a hoisted position ha-side of himself.. Holding the bike like a phone.. Brian grins still considering in himself the possibilities between 2 types coincidences' and the perfect timings'..

"Bring-Bring-bring me a world of .. May I take your order? Brian spins the wheel of the bike closest to his reach ..apeer-ing to eyeball nothing with no focus at all and echoes into the wheel as it fans the breeze that smooths through the park with ease..

She leans towards him. "Did it respond? What did it say? Is anything there?"

He laughs and spins the wheel again as he sets the bike back down.. "Oh, OK.. So, I don't think that.. Maybe, nothing responded.."

The girl questions Brian like a smashed pumpkin that regrets spoiled seeds and she inquires as if it really mattered. "What the hell do you mean? Maybe, nothing responded?"

"Oh well.." says Brian "If i could sell you an abandoned barn and on the receipt I could remind you to pray for Jesus as a tax relief fund.. Would that be a compliment for me or them or anybody?"

She shouts back- "You're not making sense."

"What's the difference between nonsense and perfect sense?" -Brian trials "Sometimes I think I'm not a person.. Just a thing.. Sounds like I just lost my job.. I think I'd fire you for fake problems that peddle sneaky suspicions.."

Pool'd over

Candid sights for sore eyes as Brian wakes to find himself slowly aware of where he is.. He rolls off the couch onto the floor as a blanket wrapped around his leg drags and pulls against his purpose into a relinquished stretch.. Crawling a bit to reach an old TV sitting on the desk..

The TV snaps a loud hiss as he reaches to turn the volume down.. Perhaps that.. He thought he would just test the thing and see if it was even plugged in.. Flipping through the channels that may have been worth watching.. But the static appeared to blink and fade as though the tuning ability was not a possibility.. Looking toward the living room he could see the bike near the door.. The TV then tuned a channel suddenly in a static wave of a war movie of some sounds and explosions.. Then it seemed to be re-channeled to another strange sound that was more war effects as the picture puzzled in pixelated waves until.. Brian switched the old tube off from its streamlined crunch of viz-hoo-walled-buzz.. Diluted static of the early sunlight barely creeping into the house ..

As Brian found this morning morally fused with thoughts and his eyes still bugged from a vexed and temporarily troubled insinuation.. Like the wilded history pointed through the known entrapments of the rude instances of intuition.. It was .. About long enough to hear the screen door squeak as Brian was looking at the bike on the porch and snagging up his backpack.. He looked back at the old TV as it was a reminder of.. another times' taste of sharing what they love.. A war machine'd of mastery for the "tuff as nails" propaganda.. that seemed to be intact.. Perhaps there are the best moments in our lives .. If you were a Radiostar ..you would remember them.. with a killer's scent of question.. They say that.. And many things in life are like riding a bike.. Once you have.. you should know what to expect.. As the money reasons they war to hymn as he was.. that he found that.. riding a bike was better than walking.. To what we thought.. when it comes to traveling the commune of now-here in particular to go.. And so..

Riding any direction into somewhere he had never been was a home to how a moment felt to Brian when he had thought of it. Riding west would be ok for at least 1000 miles or so and so.. Could put some wind beneath the rubber and reflectors slapped with paint.. All secured to go.. And all together and over a moment that became a day-long ride into the road that reads like western philosophy made from a scientific emotional displacement.. or even like a new flavor for a baked potato experiment ..about power conditioning.. At minimum the equation tenders availability into conveniences with a gas station at the end of every sentence.. And as he slowed to a stop and let the bike rest to the wall of the side of the station.. He reaches into his bag to recover the empty water bottle and strolls tired into the store with everything as it should be.. and as if it was all a meant to be.. a mistake of perfection about the beautiful side of a blind faith..

A voice laughs up a comment from nowhere .. "You look as beat as a ripe sweatband".. The brickwall reads a tag made for the omage of the past tense from a cheap paint-can sprayed like..

"BLOoD SWeaT and Road Dust.."

A method of house warming for the taught mindset in the art of path making insights.. Something like the recognition of how or who may be making dust and or eating it.. and what all that could mean.. And the sound of a voice that seemed to scratch the focus from the way he listened and sharp as fresh air..

"I may have imagined myself about a million times over all of these sumtioned ways of could be, like persuading in the chances of happenstances'." -The voice troubles..

"What the?" Brian looks around for a voice.. what sounded like a ripoff that decided to go pro haircut.. Brian's eye's blink 182 until he can see a stringy being of a man of who's voice somewhat exploited the time and space continuum .. "Are you the DJ or something?" Brian asks as he fills the water bottle from the walls' nozzle outside the dead-head of a gas station..

The man appears to crawl a bit from around the side of a dumpster.. seeming to fit between the glare of the sun about the shadows and the steel structuring of the huge monstrous.. been there before..

"Awkward in any case.." The man mutters to and about. "Does this mean the store is closed?" The man asks the kid.. and laughing like a toy gun from the 70's sounds ..

"Better watch out for that hoes' water kid.. If I could.. I would warn ya about that.. That shit is dirty" ..

Brian sidesteps .. "I think maybe.. That maybe.. the parents could be over-rated.." Brian twists the water faucet and relinquishes it with slogs and chugs..

"So is that the case they gave ya?" The creature of a man hops down to the ground. "I don't see how I could be the DJ.. But, I think people do.. I mean.. a.. they do sometimes call me the potato man.."

The old man gasps and roars a chuckle. "Yeah sometimes life is a well processed incentive that has a long shelf life .. Then the nother somebody will be telling you to avoid the processed foods, but then making sure you take a multivitamin.. What the hack did they get a vitamin from? Vitamin trees? Every since people been working with the computers they can't find reality enough to afford the appearances.. Are you one of those new age hacker kids?"

Brian squints back into the sun setting.. "New age? I think maybe I could be."

"Well than skip a license and work for free .. dumb!" The potato man cracks off gaspin laughs wide open.. "Do ya Get it? FREE DUMB! Ha ha .."

Hacker Brian stairs off. "If how I looked was the judge of how I felt .. it might be as valuable as scratching a cute coochie or something..?"

"Well why wouldn't it be? Nothing is free is what they say but.." answers the man as Brian continues staring off.. "The insinuation would be socially a no Profit margin.. I think maybe I should feel lucky but I don't want to enjoy it.. I mean.. What's lucky? Is it up to me or is society deciding about it all?.." Hacker Brian contests as if trying out for the misfits .. "What's my luck? Who decides the lucky rules?" Brian apeere'd to demand a response..

The potato's voice groans a bit.. "Well, if you aren't sure then just don't say anything.. it could be that crazy sound garden as the poor people comply by raging against the machine.."

Pool'd over

The sound of a large truck seemed to hover around Brian and rumbling the ground as the truck parked close to the building where Brian was sleeping under the old 10 speed.. He had leaned it against the back-wall.. The rims and bike frame war like bars of his cage and he looks up from the protection of his double hooded sweatshirt to see a person in the cab of the delivery truck moving around and then the door pops open.. and a fog of cigarette smoke puffs about the air mixed with the organic stankolang of burning diesel..

The driver looks at the young man stooped from his sleep.. "Hey.. You hungover or just a wanderer?"..

The short driver lights up a cigarette and offers any cigs for Brian with a common persisting wake up offering.. "I wouldn't have parked so close but I didn't see ya.. All I saw was the bike.." ..

Brian waves a half cared motion laying back down into stillness.. "Yeha, I'll smoke it in a minute.. just leave one on the ground.."

The driver drops a couple of cigarettes on the ground next to the bike tire.

"Hey man, you want a coffee?" ..The man offers.. "I make serious custom coffee and cream and I got it with me.. I make it .. I call it.. The Great Moses..

Brian moans.. "No ma.. schools out for summer.."

But, the Driver crabs on .. "Common you gotta try this one mate.. What's ya name?" The driver reaches into the truck and tosses a fresh papercup toward Brian and the cup bumps off the rim spokes of the bike as a rolling, hollowed sound next to him.. He then he reaches to pick up the cup..

"It's just you, the cheap loner bike riding champ?" The man asks in the pretense of intent as a shared sonic youth..

"The Great Moses.." Brian repeats back grinning like a spin doctor and leaning up more and sitting up..

"Yeah Well.." Marks' back the man.. It's just milk and honey.. But this is my favorite.. this blueberry honey.. It's your lucky morning Mate! Man you gunna love this!"..

"Blueberry honey?" Brian's tiredly interests wake'd him as he pushed the bike to the side and scoots into a sitting slaggard.. then rubbing his eyes as the driver digs around the truck for somethings'..

"Well I never.. Heard.. anybody complain.. about a Great Moses in any form that I make it.. I decided this combo is the big blue virgin.. So, I guess it would be more rightly the.. The Big Blue Moses.. Maybe that sounds too much, but it was originally that.. I made it.. the milk and honey coffee Moses with blueberries.. but then I found this blueberry honey and I am in love.."

The driver pours between hot water and other things and turns with cigarette smoke foo fighting from under the lid of his hat.. Handing out another paper cup that looked stolen the same as a service station's style.. And Brian takes it and fits the cups together to double the insulated morning moment.. He sneezes and coughs and holds the heated cup in front of his face like a powerful source or force of inspirations'..

"Smells very sweet. Yeah man.. Have you ever put nothing in it?" -Brian

"Nothing?" the driver puffs more foo-fights like a blues traveler..

"You know.. Weed?" Brian insists in a question as if the burning bush was just found or something..

The driver flinches a bit.. "Weed ain't nothing.. But, Yeah that's the way to do it though."

Brian leans in feathering through like a wallflower.. "Oh, so weed ain't nothing? Well, then if weed ain't nothing.. What is weed?"

The man coughs back.. "OMG kid, Now you're getting intuit.. Wondering around the ideas of socially intrepid moral aptitudes are about knowing the seen and unheard. But its not about suicide... Its a hanging gesture man.. but not suicide.. If you ask me ..about moral aptitude in society.. or what you should assume.. It's out the window kid.. but its not about suicide.. "

Brian interrupts lagged by the might in the bosstone.. "Who said anything about suicide?"

The driver trumps back.. "I don't know .. I'm just saying.. Heartburn is a flavor like hurt feelings.. Why do you think they go to church for? Milk and Honey? Your guess is as good as mine.. it's OUT THE WINDOW KID" - The drivers voice seemed to trail off..

Brian thinks off and about.. as the diesel plumes blurbed the sense of it all feeling like an empty candlebox..

"What the heck makes ya think I'm talking about suicide?" Brian asks and looks up.. and as a moment flies by the way they say it does.. He realizes he is still sleeping in the same place under the old 10 speed bike as a stream of morning light had begun to warm the front of his hoodie that had been hooded over his face.. And nobody was around..

It is possibly assumed that Moses paid by spreading the waters and walking in the path of righteousness and as the light formed a brighter bulbous blue glow.. Brian jumped up and packed out with the road as a highway built for machines made of heavy throttles and hard trusts.. The pavement reflected the paths of the rocky bed of truths padded from the insolations between the sky's qualms ..with the earth.. An element of guiding farthest from bias is.. English as concepts.. it is what it sounds like.. As if your opinions really matter.. And of course in the highest ways of pretension.. This guy would sustain to say that luck happens.. But luck can't be explained.. or else it wouldn't happen.. A functional forget about it ..on an auto-piloted sense of conclusions for timeless advices.. that can't come in a rush.. Do you need to find the roots of commune? Don't ask the auto-pilot for directions.. Sometimes you got all the luck and.. Could be the luck had.. Choose.. Punchlines that rude the power of choices because society is wired to the tune of a time manipulation.. for a machine of used shoes.. A Radio Fantasy.. Or that's what some may say ..and that people want to be heard.. and or if they hurt.. Or perhaps for those of whom prefer not to worry as comfort in the absence of social awarenesses'.. That obscure highway of annoying insights as the wind bolds your eardrums and you decide finding keychain items scattered as nothing is a new creative hobby.. Spare change is a comforting incubus of the verve in the goo-goo-dolls time costing resources.. Wherever Nirvan is found in the tunes of social stamina as they stall and or stunt..

Suddenly Brian is tagged out from his hypnotic tethering the lines between the gravel and smooth of the grooves by the sound of a vehicle from the side slowly..

"Maybe kids shouldn't be riding bikes on the highways.. " Says the officer from his patrol car as he smooths cruze beside the peddled ease Brian had slowed too..

"What? I'm not a kid" says Brian ..

"Teenagers are kids.." The officer smarts back ..

Brian stalls a moment and peddles onward.. "yep.. ok teenagers are the kids"

"But you're not a kid.. as far as riding a bike.. I'd say teenagers aren't kids if we are talking about riding bikes .. Right?" The officer obviously humorously amused at the nobody young man from who knows where..

"OK OK.. I'd say a teenager that rides a bike is still a kid.. but it's not a childish thing to do.." Brian states as he continues riding with the oasis of a radiohead..

"It's not?" the officer asks and laughs "oh yeah, of course not.. Well don't ask me what I know about it.. as far as society being a kid at heart and all that.. But resourcefully .. Everything is all about sex.." -cop

"Everything is all about sex?" -Brian asks back to the soul asylum..

"Well kid.. I did not complain about.. them thinking that ..How I live on donuts.. They don't pay me to explain that stuff you know.. so I gotta go.." The officer drives off forwardly with horse powered propulsion and Brian looks around and suddenly.. As Brian laid there listening and realizing he had found the faith no more side of social propaganda.. just woken up.. from some strangely loud muffler dodging dingo of a car.. crushing it in the twilight of the nowhere traveled highway.. RAmbling an echo of fading grace as Brian rolls over and looks past the sleep in his eyes to see some tail lights simmering from the sights of no-doubt.. The tics and tacs of bugs flighting around the light from above the side of the wall tickled like the lemonheads and as he had a real sneaky craving for hot coffee .. of which insinuates a brief lag of waking .. but most dudes can breath as easy as the sun rises.

"Somebody stole all the insulation to the walls in your apartment.." A voice cobbles from a far sound..

Brian looks around to find the potato man mimicking to be feeling around with his arms waving like a stoned hippie in the stoop of a p-p-dance.. As if looking for the walls of his apartment or something..

"What the hell are you talking about?" Brian cranks back.. "Did you tell that car to wake me up?" Brian strains to look around.. "Yo.. Potato man.. get a job! Listen man.. You got a serious superstition about virgin stained Jeans like the chaba cubra tattoos memorabilia taboos .. about nothing to be specific.. it's Deja voodoo..." -Brian

"Kids are always trying to get away with anything all the time.." The potato man chats on. "You ask'm and they say.. I'm not doing nothing.. That's, that nothing in denial strategy you know.. and strategy sounds like tragedy and.. And which one is more like sugar? Gas or Weed?" -potatoman

"You sound like sugar BURN!" Brian counters like an accounting crow..

"It's as peculiar as an awkward Beetle's fan who's co-dependent on stale pizza.. I'm serious man.. You better get these walls checked.." The potato man insists as he points around non-directionally stooped..

"So, you're the building inspector all of a sudden?" Brian questions "How the hell are you working for the company of contemporary free-dumb?"

"Just because it's free doesn't mean it's worth anything!" -The potatoman fans from the gallery..

"Well.. Fucking-free!.. free! is really confusing to make sense of.." -Brian thinks out-law'd..

The riding on roads and paths can seem forever in a day of inspiration..

Pool'd over

Beaded lights strung as rows that far off into society's wastelands like a deep end of more and more pasts' by.. and as the day of light dries to the end of a bottled water..

"You shouldn't ride your bike out here.. These people are terrible drivers.." a voice comes from over the scenes rebelling buzz.. A patrol officer idles near and traffic seems nowhere as Brian looks over..

"Yeah well the building inspector asked me to check and see if these roads are properly connected to the ground.." says Brian as he slows to a no handed travel and points around.. "Flighty issues or something.. And competency issues about.." Brian shouts over the windy engine noise like a moment..

"Social scarcity experiments!" -Brian

"Yeah, I guess that's a cool band name.. I don't know if that's illegal or not .." -the cop hooties like a blowfish.. "But you look like you are enjoying it.. Pedestrians as refugee's? Might be brewing a crazy fight of passage that I don't have time for.. with stirring blends of excuses.. Yeah, keep on top of that!"

The officer drives off punching the gas as if kicking dust was a good omen.. And why shouldn't it be.. Ever since we had that conversation about talking to god, she's been out of it.. Feminized safety concerns for a forgotten public that has a crazy opinionated community of phone number based calamity.. Even racist as if .. like blue collar eating the green collards.. and the never ending palette of white lying.. and all other types of punk'd assed colors.. The times of the hack-knee-Yuppies and Prank callers .. Technologically as trust hides as queer as straight grey.. Can money make the power lose its place amongst the pennywise of it all?

As if there is a difference..

Many people think of DeJaVu as a state of disorientation while others understand DeJaVu as a point of Ecstasy. Livid forms of interpretive information as microbitted and conforming id-iom-rhythmicly as surrounding conceptual motives.. Cumulative commerces con-geniously interplay.. Subversive, subconscious awarenesses preconceived as notions related of and or, about.. being itself.. Spiritually paranormal as conversation for and or from the considerable capacity of interests perpetuated as "DARE-ELECTS".. I have to be a representative?

Retrospect in question.. The manual appeared to say that.. The Building inspector insisted that amongst the collective soul..

I wouldn't be able to imagine if the standards war real or not.. And so with these preiminated iniquities regarding the will of god over mans' wheel. And of mans' will for himself.. Mans' harvest of the lost focus within hymn and self is an infinite love.. For the love of mans' wheel and hiss.. wheel.. with or without god as the emotive equivocation of indifferences'.. That love ensures an elevation of conceptual tune towards man's experiences of being "on high".. And what the farm remembers to forget .. De-Ja-Vu-doooo.. Could be subrooted effects of anti-intelligent and or religious techno-city.. About the auto-intelligenivism.. Tauted habitual phrases and or conservative motivations of questions that may amount of promoted ideals as associative taboos.. As this circus of the lord god needs hu.. to witness reality as a generally regulated moderation and introspective as hymn self and of selves.. In a multi-peer-son-owl.. Obtrusive and merciful melancholy of dignity and integrity for altruism with self recognizability for messenger services.. As euphemism and innuendo tango the carousels in the pinball machine specialized like a game to measure up to some refining of rude skills.. Perhaps the funk shunned and nobody needed to catch some air.. These questions of contamination staminized conversation with a stimulative outcome that I found.. Do you feel like you are doing what you supposed to be doing?..” Brian asked himself as the peddles wound in a rhythmatized road of reflection..

A truck drives passed Brian and a person waves and shouts something out the window.. The pickup truck then swerves back to turn around swerving to and from the lanes as a voice shouts..

“Stop! it’s dangerous man! you can’t ride your bike across the highway.. You better stop!”

The man swerves his truck blocking both lanes of the highway.. and Brian stops as the truck had been parking blocking the lane like an instantaneous minor threat.. Brian decided to stop.. Still not interested in the concern’t about having to stop riding on the highway.. So, he put the bike down and walked up to the truck as the man in the truck began to get out of the truck.. Brian makes a comment about not being interested in old queers with sneaky suspicions for young boys and grins as he puts his foot up on the truck door pinning the man between the door and the truck.. The man was 10 or 20 years older and at least 100 pounds bigger..

“I don’t think... you can ride bikes on the highway..” The man struggled for a moment acting surprised by Brian and the aerosmith of the moment..

“I don’t think? What was that?” Brian sharped back with a smile as he pressed to trap the man ..

“No.. you’re not supposed to be riding a bike on the highway..” The man says as he stunts..

Suddenly Brian let hiss foot down.. and as the man seemed to fall forward from Brian’s foot moving suddenly..

“I don’t think?” asks Brian out-law’d..

The man was off balance, a great moment for Brian to squarely surprise the larger man with a mighty clobber of a smack.. A right whoook.. that had been like an upper cut for Brian to reach just right.. But it was a really quality smack as Brian used a closed fist type to seal the deal.. There are a patagonia of smacks and struts depending on who's in a smacking contest with who.. A solid connection can be a very brief moment of intimacy.. Sometimes there's a little blood, but if you have to get in a fight with a man twice your size.. regardless of innuendo.. You will get a better ringing in your ears knowing you clocked the mother fucker a good stunt before he gets a chance to stop and ask you the square root of 5 times the world's debt.. And maybe that sounds very irish.. but I really crooked his jaw, a good one.. Divided by other current events and worldly blunders that compliment my irish composure as an english born creature.. ..Questions that impressed the destruction of places like the tower of babylon.. I'm sure they didn't need a tow truck to foresee the young loose cannon like oversight.. Sometimes you're not trying to be a hero.. You just don't have anything to lose.. thankfully.. The story still sounds funny in jail..

In jail with hurt feelings that nobody wants to forget about.. if this is a market value.. I wondered..

Laced shoes and chain smokers are a standing rank.. ok because they can't use.. weed.. And with the based values in question.. and they confessed about feeling lost with speedy thoughts.. I never saw these cute chicks carrying the loaded secrets as the officer chain smoked the enlisted men.. But these trumps are the stamination acting on an incentive for power that doesn't exist like they worked for the cops and the drug dealers as a hobby.. As if the Brand names knew me personally for the making of bad brains.. Who, apeered against what is right for a vigilant purpose of silent nights that war anything but.. Holistically, and self sabotage even.. but they seemed to get a stunt of power about yelling nothing about moral aptitude.. Raving in the way a street kid tiptoes past a stumbled broken bottle.. Like, the dude yelling at me from his window.. But.. that's a lame example.. because he was wrong!

Well, Judge! I'm not trying to understand what's happening around here.. don't mind me.. to tell hu.. that dude about some smack about smack.. *Those* girls don't think until you have a joke about washing your eardrums from the inside out.. Letting me live.. but then I'm the evidence of morally motivated disruption.. Compared about a drug slanged as smack.. Speeding as an excuse to see the wrong side of purpose.. Poured into the case of a soldier catching some of the left field laws't.. White people aren't so bright.. Especially, if you look like a cheap white kid.. And if you happen to be nobody.. this lord has a real thing for throw-offs.. Like ya story about a mix up.. Perhaps, that.. she thinks.. but she got shoe'd up.. Regarding a secret purpose to have government controlled by white people.. Because of some hyper focused forms of organizational feddish.. maybe.. white people are easier than organizing other people.. Or better at organizing? And because english is so easy to learn and understand.. and because white people are so stupid.. Perhaps, this was so funny enough of a conspiracy.. As defiance of nothing if nobody noticed such a paranoia.. Powers that B could.. Never B as illusive? Under the assaults of a soldier's control of checkpoints .. Beware of the governmental suck-shun of ill-commune.. That animalism of attraction trying to temper US as nothing less than moralism.. And if they raise the price of cocaine a little too much.. like heavy petty-ing.. Cooking a big meth is practically liberation swabbed from the king-dumb's dogs on a safari of sexually sufferables... I must've missed a joke about tung twisting as the godsmack lingered..

Brian tiredly stands over a sink at a truck stop service station..
Waiting for the hot water as it begins to steam up .. The station is
busy and men are in and out of the restrooms as Brian hogs the
sink near the wall.. A hippie shower isn't a recipe in the *anarchist
cookbook* because it's not that mysterious or shocking as Brian
rinses his sox and the rest of the Dharmatology with the simple
standard of wall gods soap.. Indoctrination of pink-floyd'd
devotees relies on the truck stops that are Americanized as bath
parties for pedestrians exploring the not so un-exploited question
of the broken ass.. that may or may not need fixing.. The wall gods
provide soap.. If the crew that runs the meat factory is concerned..
As if the chucks are aware of the hearsay in the scent of fart jokes..
Like social phenomena scrubbed from a plotted controversy.. Is
that a spot of consumable implication as super soluble? Rinsed
against a point of no return.. A consumable complication.. and
as this insinuation is the actions speaking louder than words..
and then also implicated with more and more of the actions..
and then also more and more of the words.. A traveler is as dumb
as dust.. Just like water in the bubble bath of a lost love for the
public that gets excited about a silly question.. But hymn really
needs a more respectable option.. As if they would know that
a lost connection and effect-shun had the differences' between
a radio and a television. Black flagging the commune of mental
stronghold.. A carefully counterfeited exchange of Karma.. Like
a Freudian force that pan-handles the technology of a used kaws..
As if life was a dirty bucket made to give dust a bubble bath as a
contradiction .. it.. must've had a headache when considering the
differences between playing ball and buying a new pair of jeans..
Like asking the purpose for money.. Divided by the printed and
stamped reasons to cut the cheese.. She's got a jealousy problem
and another thought considers how peace will find a pie.. A
petty stigma with her old revelation reminding US to send a

postcard.. Maybe he just didn't have an address for the boat.. My best wishes in regards to the absent invitation.. Seems like the used kaws war safer then buying a condom after reconsidering the hole view.. The sox looked clean enough and after rinsing his shirt he sloppe'd back outside bare-footed and slicked into his shoes and hoodie'd for a shirt.. Considering, if there was a well known science of not feeling so good.. Who would know who wasn't invited to convey it? Perhaps, it was published about the *Peanuts* man.. Or maybe at least to hope you find it.. So, you can earn the right to squat.. They say that I should be able to.. A bridge that I guess was burned for a statutory purpose before the dawn of the space age..

"I have the right to squat?" asks Brian to himself and looking around as he steps out to the outside of the truckstop and the bike was still there and looking great as the chrome reflects like rusty train tracks that'd been polished by the time it takes to make society a professional screw-up.. As if a screwy personality started a farmers' thought that maybe lazier fielding could mean less taxes.. or for whatever it was.. as the trucks were all packed and stacked around with puffs and punches of sounds that plumed gasps of coincidences like comradery on the football team.. A guy only as high.. Has high hopes for the dignity of the public as he wall-ow's through the hole-ow'd depth of a dirty bucketed suspect of equations'.. Improve is better than live TV.. But you can't remember why.. because you never wrote it down.. Wrapping the wet sox around parts of the handle-bars as a purr-affect method to squeeze another several heals from the solar air dryer cycling.. Re-filled and soaked and soaped to the degree of an escape artist's steeze..

The fresh debri that scatters the roads and bends like a personality funktion of hazard becomes a beautiful defiance of any insinuation of blind faith.. Privately, I think.. Lucky is how it rolls around yer head like symbolic subordination.. And for whatever reasons' they make cough syrups in cherry..

Maybe that will cool it off as the fire marshals contemplate those organic notions against the limits of abilities of the natural time.. Considering the material farfegnugen..

The wifi CODE

They say many things are like riding a bike and by such a meaning of that.. They meant many things about balance and ability to track between the need to know and the don't ask and don't tell suspects of equations.. Because, what I don't know.. and the urge to subordinate the embellished dividends.. Multiplied by the admirations of the money it made to export the algebra of common mysteries.. And as the accountants are everything as nothing types of conscious control.. with common sense like honey from the bee-hive.. of how society is an inviting emotional disaster with the attorney as hiss.. Screaming uncle with a white lung.. Implications of anything other than a tragedy case might make them get uncomfortable.. and you might ask that.. them.. to give a fuck about how they feel.. As a native of King Dumb in the urban assaults of point blank.. Looking around as a social comparison compounded of communismistical superstitions.. As if what you don't know.. can't.. heard you..

For those of US with enough incentive in self preservation to peddle around roadsides.. and as if peasants war getting rubbed the wrong way.. Steering through the lot of like.. like a reprimand for technologies of a used kaws.. From the evolutionary values of a dirty bucket.. Considerations of why those questions appear as strokes of luck.. like watching the soapy streaks glean a spectrum of a refraction.. and that reflects a temporary promotion that pays in the form of.. attention to detail.. like a sexual innuendo during a drug induced daydream that mostly only happens if you can't recollect why.. And if the consideration was about a dirty bucket ..or if the happenstance was indifferent than those cycles.. Like or like not.. must be a common mystery in the field of taboo.. A sign on the side of the highway seemed to be a monument.. of ..as it stood 12 feet from the roadside near a small muddy drive.. Monumentalish even.. and as traffic seemed non-existent since 4 scores of miles or so.. Brian approached a site and the huge sign was older looking and weather ruffed and meddled rust.. A trench of a property behind the sign left with a hollow'd existench.. A rude memory of a brick building that remained like peaces of a puzzle that warrants being carried off by the birds.. Mostly only the foundation remaining and the rest of it had been relinquished by the mothership's purposes of iniquities..

"The STAR CHURCH" - the sign read

Also, a barn stable building that was leaning as dry as burnt grass.. The evidence of a dumpsite is the element of a very wilded and fired perch.. Maybe if "killjoy" was a pleasant scene as a mystical in the face.. for the weary travelers impressions.. "silent but deadly".. is in question regarding the reflection of the published authors that haven't officially entered the christian religion.. Denial clown is a blindside that stinks like Wisconsin cheese on your favorite peach.. And if I had some.. Perhaps, I could say I never saw a serious flavor cheese.. as if any of that cheese wasn't serious? But it's not all sharp.. Ask the dead kennedys.. seriously.. I think that.. The farm's natural abilities assume the craving and hunger to humer the commodities of a speechless trend.. Whatever of the conveniences of a futuristic world that complements the sequences' of events'.. or as another word.. Whatever I can do to avoid square-dancing to the tune of bed credit.. Tax season always hurts me like the first time.. Every time.. Nothing is on the scales and I'm a blind selfie discovering social stigma by stressing in the airwaves.. like a shat in the park but you don't have a dog.. And you ask yourself about what you think you would be able to do.. These marketing bots that fathom the patterns of micro-traktion like original as a barbershop.. They apologize about the way they stick to yer shoe.. or how a thumb feels when it's pressed into your eyeball.. Like fake dignity.. As if that helps.. You can't be having these games that aren't supposed to exist.. In my city it's illegal to act fake while holding a guitar.. Obviously, because that case would be hilarious! As if you could prove that your mental problem is about you having a difficulty explaining your problems.. "scizo".. If it was as easy as saying your dogs are your feet.. Like that archetype of you-in-a-verse-hall.. I think in question of contrary, complexion.. Encyclopedias should be more right and Dictionaries are a libral sanctuary.. Living in a space'd age as a quality nobody you might feel as untraceable as second hand smoke.. If you're lucky then the others will never have to feel bad for you.. Society is the peer-effect absent invader of professionalism.. She's the sugar and He's the salt.. The story rocks the voices in my head.. dub-hole dosed as an impression about an emotional toll service that intends to avoid terrible introductions.. like a stolen bike or like a cold shower.. terrible introductions can be like voices that wouldn't ever be heard.. unless there was a problem.. and there better not be.. and for whatever reasons.. they make the cough syrups' in cherry..

"talk-sick-city" is an emotionally thwarted recording.. As like I said.. when dealing around the hackers' presumptions' of the 'coincidences'.. spelled like a grudge-matched insinuation and leading as a casual denial.. As if it wasn't meant to be.. All the yeah yeah yeah's could've been a real happenstance.. Although, premeditated definitions for "coincidences" may appear casual.. About how these 2 types of coincidences become one.. As innuendo swings through the relationships of the definitions.. "goin-psy-dance"

I'd say, I must've been smoking that.. stuff..

Perhaps, of a standing recollection.. So we can intrigue a certain reaction.. perhaps to call back all kour descendents for a trip with trigonometry.. Vaguely though many claim they are trying mythical sexual positions and moves as clever revivals to the point of laughing at the prowess of faith.. of society's fancy hearsay like scapegoat policies.. Intentions well considered as far as.. a breaking ball at midnight.. Hit or miss was both an oragy.. some types of co-in-si-dances war intended.. and some war not.. And the bio-bubbles said that.. The lord farmed man from that.. does'd.. happenstances' of sex-heel relations could not be proved nor disproved? These cards are people as mass conceptual guests' of histories sultry pasts'.. While realizing if yours matter'd or not.. A foul contention that leans towards the impressions that others can claim.. Learn't..

Some others have more time then more others? Ask the wall gods..

They would tell you that the answer is in the directions of the recipe for the soap.. or maybe the dispenser..

If they could admit to remembering.. what the fuck a pub was for..

Brian scuffs around the site of the .. that was no more..

"The Star Church" -a voice says..

A voice cringes from the rafters of the barn as Brian wonders around.. "Well, this one time, I thought that I should be dead and that.. also.. I wasn't sure if it was a good thing that I was still alive." Gloats a voice roosting the sparrows from the bugbites..

"Ask that dude if that's a hard truth.." Brian says as he laughs.. "Is that a hard truth hiding in the waste of it all, Potato-man?"

As if getting the voices confused was a point of contact.. Brian finds himself realizing that the afternoon was close to the end.. and the barn area being calmed as clear from the prairie winds..

"I think you gotta fight for your right to feel right.." the potato man coughed out as he appeared to be set up in a rafter of the barn beyond a shadow of a doubt..

"Well, maybe believing is for suckers and they don't want me to feel right.." Says Brian as he sets his stuff around and the bike down'd in the corner of the barn with the sun setting and still warming the old cracked and dry boarded test of time... "Cause whenever the fights over .. if ever.. I'll be all sore and brewzed and beet-up about it.. and then who of who is the comparison for what?" And as the rays of light lazered around the dust and the plumes of the prairie winds and the comfort of the warmth radiating a stable wall of the inside of the dry and dusty sense of reality.. Brian sluffed into a sleepiness..

Wondering in research on a lifestyle.. built like an eat and run charade.. And as Brian is slowly noticing that.. of an indifferential view of the world like learning that sunday traffic is an all encompassing compromise of all of a sudden.. all at the same time.. The city is an emotionally thwarted recording.. As like they said.. and as the discretion of the ages dissolves with the time it takes to have a dream..

The Truck Fight

"I wasn't trying to kick anybody.. I was just running to the next base!" A sounds murmur as Brian looks up .. He reminds himself to remember where he is going.. Just barely missing another light post.. Swerving into the cityscape wrapped around him.. he slows to stop near the man who looked like an imaginations' sour creation of bitterly contained.. The short man war a grin and stirred back quickly with his cigar smoldering in the chilli air..

"Are ya just riding a bloc?" -the man laughs loud and breathes through the moonlight frags of the pearl jam..

Brian grins back and cluelessly responds as confident as nobody could and nods.. "Yeah.. a bloc.. maybe that's what.. it did.. but then.. that wasn't what it was about.. Was it?."

The short man laughs harshly and then appears to cough up a lung just like how they say it happens.. Laughing through the lung toss like a well trained survival seminar.. Brian thinks the old short man must fetch a chili moment of humor on the steps rather normally.. as it was.. The man continued bulgering..

"This life is such a gamble.. I think they should make the dashboard do light shows after you fill up with premium fuel.." The man gasps back to the conversation and wiping the tears from his face and giggling..

"I think that mine did!" -Brian snaps.. realizing he was being clever on the spur of a moment..

"Next thing you know .. people will be so hypnotized by the dashboard.. then they'll be thinking that they are check-engine lights!" The gung ho goose-necker blabs on.. "I think they made crazy.. a profession.. but the excuse is that they war just trying to help me.." the man laughs.. "That Charles Manson guy thought he was a check engine light.. But don't ask me to prove that though.."

"Aren't we all referees or somethin?" Brian asks as he lights a cig... "Maybe I need an interpreter to see the meanings in the considerations about how to use a cigarette?"

The old guy chuckles and swofts a hand into his pocket and pulls an apple that looked rather crisp.. Suddenly a blackbird that had been branched across the street caws at the sight of an apple in the old man's hand.. "wise that?" asks the man.. The bird argues sounding consciensiously..

Brian puffs a bit back.. "uh hum .. you know cause I don't know, what other people think.."

"What? Well, of course you do.." The man arg's him and crunches a bite from the apple..

"I do?" says Brian "Yeah, maybe if they think it's all a video game about knowing how much it's worth to know.. without knowing anything.."

The old man listens and contrives "Sometimes I think it sounds like somebody is secretly riding society's asses all the wrong way and then that um.. Whatever it's worth amounts to jokes about foreign concepts.."

"foreign to me?" -Brian

"It's like how wearing suits transformed into a different meaning and the common perspective of a clown has always been in question.. more or less or not.. Some cultures actually have.. social rules about touching your ass with your right hand.." The old man taughts..

"What the?" asks Brian "Wait.. for real? What's the rule?"

The man laughs a chuckle.. "it's against it.."

"How did they decide that shit?" Brian asks..

"Well, it was about shit.. I know that for sure.." The old man crunches away on the apples crisp and tosses the half nawr'd apple into the grass across the street to the black bird who swoops onto it..

"So, if I touch my ass with both hands, then I'm some type of libral?" -Brian

"That'd be funny if that's what it meant huh?" -old man

"Maybe ..maybe it'd be different by the time I could ask anybody.." -Brian

"Why, you always worrying about what other people think? Any shade of truth could be real.. Have you ever had a mental problem?" -Old man

"No.. Naw.. I think maybe all I have in there is time.. What wrong could go with it? A mental problem? Naw .. it just means they cheated or something.." -Brian

The old man sits against the steps.. "I was pissed when they said I had the.. schizophrenial-whatsa.. whatever it was.." The old man pressed on..

"And I was all trying to ask'm how the hell I got the schizofractal disease.. Or where did it come from.. And you wanna know what the nurse said?.. You're not going to believe this.. She said that I was being hell'd in the mental place because I had somehow created this scizo disease!"

Brian laughs covetly as the old man continues to flood with irony..

"So.. then I was asking her.. How did I make this disease? you know.. How did I do it? and then I already knew it.. ya know .. I knew it was because I hacked my own brains.." laughing bursted from both of them laughing like a unified sucker league camping the beaches of coastal regions..

The bird across the street flinches up to notice the 2 shared a jane's addiction type of humer and the old man continued..

"And then I was asking the nurse if they had tried lemonade in hot water as a way to stress the scizophractal disease.. but I was really.. just wondering if they could get me some ritalin or some adderall most of the time.. You want some coffee?".. asks the old dude..

"Huh, coffee? right now?" Brian flicks the cig and jumps to question.. "But how did you hack your brains? Are they still hacked? How can you tell if your brains are hacked?" -Brian

The old man jumps up.. "Well, at first I thought that I should be able to remember.. but then I also realized I could only hack my brains from a remote source.. And then I can't remember what that means.. or wait .. it was that the subconscious self would create its own image.. and I can't fathom it.."

"What a cop-out.." -Brian

"That's tha truth.. like achieving a particular destination of interest by dumpster diving" The man rants on..

"It's like this.. When you're a 50's kid like me.. house broke is a lifestyle.. for hindsight.. about how to undermine the intelligence of public domain.. then there gunna fill yer head with mushy crap that will make ya feel as dump as a dump.. and nobody denial is harsh on it.. trying to reject the existence of nobody without trying is almost as clever as fighting without fighting.. but this ain't the 70's.. Judges get all boggled because they can't look at it in the same light.. because the vantage point is deciding about contact sports compared to panning for gold or something.. They warrant trying not to look at it all the same though... Where's the contact? Stealing a pan or pissing in the river?"

Brian bursts with laughter and flicks his cigarette into the streets foggy blindside.. The old man appears to puff cultivated like in the moment.. The man puffs and continues..

"The sheep-dog effect-shun of the system-addict methods of passing the buck.. As an excuse to have a party in an unexpectable place or way or something.. Raving! like cats and dogs.. and then you see that ..they shit differently.."

Brian chuckles asking- "Who, shits differently?.. Differently than me?"

"The muddy side of the pan handle.." the man rules on.. "And some things you don't want to prove.. but then the fish just swim in it.. That's something weird about seafood culture and.. I think it proves cats must be able to hypnotize people.." -man

"The cats.." puffs Brian.. "Yeah, I think I believe in that.. my mom did have a cat.." Brian sherks..

"Have you ever seen a cat near the ocean?" asks the man as the smoke fills the view like guns and roses packs the seats...

"They won't be able to blame communism this time.. but, the cornerstone of nothing is the nobody incentive.. Some people are just nobody's but .. what do they think about it?.. When they don't realize that they are nobody? Because the revelation of being nobody.. Maybe, did.. happen.. Presumably.. but they wanted to forget about that.. being nobody.. or feeling that way.." Echoes the old man as he stepped off and caw-feeing from the alley..

"As a civil respect I'd have to say.. they are lazy as a definition that scapegoated from seeing themselves as a definition.."

The old dude seems to bounce off the ground in expression after reappearing into sight.. "You need to realize what kind of nobody you are.." -old dude

Brian listens and sparks another cigarette .. "So, I gotta know my place in nobody's nothing.."

"Yeah, but it's not even nobody's.." -oldman

Brian contends- "I think get it.. But some people never travel farther down the street then the mailbox.." Brian transgresses.. "But.. I never had a mailbox!"

"You know how they made golf? " -Asks the man

"Let me guess.. Nobody knows.." -Brian

The old guy tail whips the conversation.. "It was something he couldn't get off his mind about how .. he didn't want to have to run.. but he wanted to have a reason to go far a walk.. The no running was mostly what sold the yuppies.. So, what was the thing he couldn't get off his mind? Getting a hole in one is as easy as scoring on the first date? He was shook in the value of temporary.. Cracker-jack'd of consideration of the case of a public that should thrive in the instant of temporary.. as a superior in a contrast about how things.. just don't last.. My case Cusses and slacks like.. look man .. trucks don't drive themselves.. it would never be the truck's fault.. I think I need to lavish in the superior value of now.. like the temporary self it serves timelessly.." -oldman

Brian grins up at the stone aged steam puffs the man fumes.. "Naw.. it's a birdie if you score when you meet.. or wait.. What's the hole in one?.." -Brian

"But.. if she is the truck and he's the car ..then what's the chilli garage jokes all about?" -Old dude

Sounds like WEee are the garage.." -Brian

"Whatever .. the fuck ever.. it hisss.." The old dude cackles.. "Plenty of men have lived in a garage after they didn't split up from their wife.." the old guy giggles..

Brian cuffs the curb with his crouch- "Sometimes.. I think that society is trying not to fathom how god works.. Because.. it's superstitious about it or somethin.. exploring the fire hazards of the fantomization of socialization.." Brian takes a heavy puff.. "And I don't know why we have to drag everything out.. so heard.. all the time.." Brian cringes..

"Mindless assumptions.. superstitious about god? or superstitious about.. it? What's superstitious about what?" The old dude questions..

Brain dramatically inter-personalizes "It's not about having a better cheeseburger.. It's the interesting differences between them.. it's gotta be fair for a space avenger to say that.. girlfriends are like that.. What type of love is a roundabout method of avoiding segregation of the public's denial of the self intention?" -Brian

The old man leans to the wall and rolls his toes into his shoes and rocking back and forth.. "Well, everybody knows youngsters' intentions' are bad.. but that's a considerable notion of fear of success.. invented as a complex.. lingering around the tables of anti-existence.. Hymn-o-logically .. could be an aftermath of psychology from 2 world wars on record.. Counterfeit'd Karma could be in the questions.." -oldman

"Excuses!" Brian laughs it off..

The old man coughs a bit back and asks "OK.. I think that's it.. thats it.. A Nobody, in denial could be a safety hazard.. but.. denying nobody is totally ok? I have questions.." -oldman

Brian exclaims into nowhere.. "thats it.. thats it.." Brain flicks more ash as a breeze flups around.. "Are white people going to be the slaves of the space age world wide government?" asks Brian as a cold breeze shiverz through the fairway of the street ridden stumped ..

The old dude laughs and stares into the fog.. "Schizophrenia must be a racist thing .." -oldman

Brian retorts like an endless bottom of the barrel as a respect for improvement... "Not always sure about all that.. maybe, if we need to consider that of what might be white peoples fault as a racial contention.. but schizophrenia is definitely always the white peoples fault.. In any general sense of possible socially racist like innuendo.. "You got some ritalin?" asks Brian..

"Yeah.. all kinds!" the old dude hops back "I got a rather fancy collection actually.." -oldman

The wifi code

Brian shivers and wakes to notice he had been sleeping for a couple of hours and the chilli early morning air had begun.. The moon was bright as he leaned up and looking around.. He doubles up his other hoodie and walks into the moonlight considering if he could get serenaded like an east side sandwich.. And in the scent of the quiet place that smelled as much like nothing having its place could smell like..

"You better learn what the marriage laws mean.. before you meet too many girls these days.." the man laughs a gasp.. "Or what that means.. or exactly what .." Brian heard the potato man's voice snuck from behind a heap of nothing in the dark..

"Marriage loss?" asks Brian sounding as rancid as he could..

"Yeah, that.. what.. that.. that sounds like.." the potato man chuckles.. "Marriage loss has a great surrealism of a mud puddle like of a ring about it.. That might be one of the roots of the frantic-cawzation of the scizo-izmz.." -potatoman

"It .. gets.. bed-her.. like a private sense of silence in the gallery.. and self protection laws.. Maturity is a mindless disaster as a past time favorite or not.. People fancy the sport of forgetting your right to defend yourself.. And that comes with remembering what it feels like to sink like a rock.. embedded.. Maybe making a mess of society.. leaves a slammed door policy of guessing games in the thresh-hold of publics' dirty steps.. For some of them.. It's a great rush and others make it.. Look good by studying better falling techniques.." -potato man

"Suspiciously sounds like my kind of humanitarianismZz.." -Brian

"For elitists.. Body shocks are a tempering of special forces.. and some things really are innuendos.. They say that's how you know you went too far.. Like a dent stewing in the dark.. teeth cleanings and chiropractors are the more obvious hints about massage and messaging services.. Watcha cook'n?" -potatoman

"Cooking? I'm just going to build a little early morning campfire.." -Brian

"Well, if you're an honest hard worker.. She'll still tow-hook your swing-arm-grommet a time or 2 somehow.." -PotatoMan

"Swing-arm-Grommet?" Brian looks over to see the potato man stretching his shoulder and pointing into his armpit as the tall man temps back hopping around on one foot in a circle..

"And I don't know how things that happen to cars and trucks are later remembered as ice skating coincidences'.. or maybe thats' was a happenstances'.." potato man walks off into oblivion like he was Motley Crue all in one man..

"Happenstances? I don't know.. I heard that when people are knocking on ya.. it's supposed to make ya hungry?" -Brian

"Yeah, it gives you a headache that you really don't want to have.." -Potatoman

"Is that a thing to look forward to or.." -Brian

"I knew a blackbird that claimed to be raised stuffed.." -Potato Man

"What ya say? Erased?" -Brian

"Sometimes I just chalk it up to a smelly feet problem in the hallway of the big house.. But then if I'm talking like that .. then people start thinking I was born from a prison family with a strange humor of city's and zen and shit like that or something.."

Brian kicks some dust in an attempt to gather enough scattered twigs and trash items to make a toasty morning free like fresh air or a cheap lighter.."

"Maybe they all just have a real picky time staying questioned about the differences of cheap?" -Brian

"I love cheap stuff!" -Potato Man

".. and or if cheap is supposed to be a good thing or a bad thing.." -Brian

"Cheap has the freedom to be both!" Potato Man gripes up.. "Like maybe.. we got them equal rights to be equally poor right.. or poor wrong.. Free-dumb for that?" -potatoman

"Well I 'd say the REAL differences are between.. cheap and rip-off.." -Brian

"Well.. How poor are you? How do you prove how poor ya-are?" -Potato Man

"Yeah.. how poor is a rip-off? Maybe a rip-off isn't based on price?" -Brian

"Not all rip offs could be cheap but .. wait.. why would that be the real difference?" -Potato Man

"I thought we war trying to prove how poor you are.." -Brian

"OK, now the difference is really sounding like a rip-off.." -potato man

"Well, some things aren't worth it.. that's how you know.." Brain Exclaims "Rip-off"..

"But how do you know?" -potato man

"I think my thumbs are cheap and these fingers are rip-offs..." -Brian laughs like a white zombie..

"You want to trade your fingers for thumbs?" -potato man

"Naw, I want to trade my luck for a dime.." -Brian

"So the thumb is the luck ? Or the fingers? -Potato Man

"The thumbs is a dime and the fingers are lucky .." -Brian

"ok maybe I think.. I think they do that.. at the casino.."
-potato man

"Naw, it's not that I was trying to explain how poor I was.. or wasn't.. but mostly I was trying to avoid my life being an innuendo or something.." -Brian

"And so.. through this .. so you graduated as nothing.." potato man stomps around into a dust storm..

"I think I could follow that assumption, but there are so very many more.." -Brian

Potatoman stops spinning around and looks.. "More what?" -potatoman

"There's more assumptions..." -Brian

"Yeah well maybe you need to look at these things like cheeseburgers.. and maybe reconsider.. I mean before or.. if you didn't want to be an innuendo.." -Potato Man

"Reconsider what before what?" -Brian

The potato man seemed to flightly strut through the shadows of the boards around the barns huge dry rot of a lean.. as his voice was echoing.. "Well... why war it matter if you war an innuendo?" -potatoman

"I'm not so sure actually.. I'm not sure if I knew if it mattered .. I think Maybe I was just laughing about it.." -Brain

"an innuendo?" -Potato Man

Brian stumbles around and around and gathers up things and scattered trash for the fire and strands to think.. "Yeah.. But, then the innuendo caused me to forget again.." -Brian

"That crazy innuendo.. which one was it?" The potato man laughs..

Brian stands up and scans and keeps looking for trash for the fire..

"I think I need to make a more better collage of these innuendo's.. " -Brian

"I know all the innuendo families.. I'll have a talk with those raskals for ya.." -the potato man shouts..

"Maybe, it made me forget for a reason?" Brain answers while reaching for some twigs..

"What a Rip-off!" The potato man slams back into a gust of dust dancing around and around as the pieces of garbage that was in Brian's hands become an accumulated pile of potential morning blaze..

"Maybe, if I can remember the reason first.. and then I could recall the point of not remembering.." -Brian

The potato man fires back.. "How does an innuendo get away with that?"

Brian drops all the garbage in a spot near the barn shy of the breezed chilli gusts.. "If only an innuendo was like a cheeseburger.. Has a cheeseburger ever spit at you?" chatters off the potato man as a point of question..

Brian pulls his lighter out and exclaims.. "Yeah.. that would be a dream.. huh.." -Brian

The potato man shouts and laughs more.. "Unbelievable even.."

"Wait.. who wouldn't believe it?" -Brian

"Believe what?" -Potato Man

"Sheeeeesh" Brian sparks his lighter, troubling with the dried scraps and fluffs the first plume from the scraplings.. The flamage from the fire grew suddenly and he stacked more of the sticks over it and hoping that the fire would prove long enough to find some bigger sticks or chunks of the dry rot from the disasterdly of the Star's church..

Brian looks around for the potato man as the light flutters luminously..

"Maybe, I should.." Brian thinks and scavenges more to find some grounded pieces of dry rot..

"Huh.. what? should what?" -Potato man

"Yeah ok I think I should.. I mean.. look at it like cheeseburgers.. and these dry rot pieces of wood burn like coal.." -Brian echoes back..

"Oh Yeah.. Maybe our forefathers' did.. They say thats the fighting food.." -Potato man

"Fighting food?" Brian axes back .. "I didn't know that food could fight.."

"Yeah.. sure it does.. cause as far as god is concerned.. Nature will eat everything.." -potatoman

"*Nature*.. will?" -Brian

"Yeah.. you know .. Society is pre programmed as the coolest non-musical sucker joke.." -Potatoman

"Non-musical sucker?" Brian looks up as he has some more bigger sticks for the fire..

"It's just a little Rock and roll though.." Potato man starz air guitar-ring like a guru on painkillers..

Brian looks back towards the fire to add the gathered mix.. As he stumbles for the fire.. the flames apeere to plume strangely as the shape of the flames contend a style of translucentivity.. A figure of a person seems to show .. Somebody sitting with a signpost in one hand as if a novelty artist.. The dude has a sign that reads.. Periodic table of elements .. Brian asks the fire cat .. "What the fuck are oyu doing?" -Brian

"shhhhhssh.. don't talk to me.. I'm waiting for a chick.." Says the cat..

Brian looks around and laughs and asks.. "What? What in the hack chick are you waiting for?" -Brian

"I don't know man.." Dude cat answers back..

"You don't know?" asks Brian as the dude cat flickers about..

"Just leave me alone.. because I prepared a long time for this.." The cat slangs back as the fire crackles into a plume of pluff..

Brian drops everything and can't stop laughing.. After rolling on the ground for a moment he looked up and the morning tint had begun to bloom the sky..

"The Fire's burning out.." Shouts the potato man from beyond some wheatgrass and dust mites..

"Is that even possible?" Brian tilts his head up to see.. the fire is about as pitiful looking as a new puppy or something.. He grabs the scatter'd bigger sticks up again.. "Maybe, I just need a nice sign or something.."

The Potato man shouts out.. "Signs are for wimps.. You gotta use your voice!"

The fire flu-u-u-umed up suddenly with a mixture of wrappers and styrofoam cups and other stuff that is good to campfire .. Brian leans back waiting for the morning rising.. As it does..

"Hey .. make your own sign!" shouts Brian wandering with a question about if .. as suddenly the potato man chops on..

"That and that.. you claim you can read outloud the rules of the road like a circus freak.." -potato man

Brian falls back and gasps a moment. "Is that a compliment or an expectation?" He asks.. -potatoman

"As the example of a judge.." Shouts the potato man followed by other murmurs and quasi-mental follies that toil the inner souls temper of dwelling..

Sitting on the ground and waiting for nothing.. Brian fell back asleep next to the warmth of a white trash fueled fantasy that burned on.. burning out for his comfort.. like the incense for the field of lost love.. or at least he could say that he was thinking that.. He thought that..

She was a warm brew of junky jargon furloughing the stink of lemon diesel paradise ...

Burning out the further side about how.. your opium baby...

The Truck Fight

The judge looked overweight and as if he could have been a friendly cousin of relativity.. The equally familiar heavy man standing behind the other side of the courtroom.. The officer on duty grinned towards the judge and reading the opening statement for the case.. The Judge stopped at the officer all of a sudden and pointed at Brian..

"You are Brian?" -asks the judge

Brian leaned forward and talked .. "Yep, I am that Brian.. Um .. Your honor.."

"Shut-up.. and wait for your questions.." -the judge quicked back.. Wrinkling the paper work and then looking through the papers and shuffling them around in the air in front of the microphone .. The judge looks up at him and then back and then looks out across the room and then back at him and suddenly he asks.. "Looks like you're not from around this town.. and I don't know anything about you. Mr. Brian.. Is this the first time you have been in a courtroom for fighting?"

"No." Answers Brian .. "Um.. Sir.. Uh.. Judge.. I .. um .. never been in trouble for fighting before."

The Judge looks back at him whispering to himself and grips the papers and calls the officer over and asks a short question.. "No.. Huh?" -the judge exclaimed out loud..

Well.. Mr. Brian I could put you in jail for up to six months.. And.. or I could charge you with a penalty up to reimburse the court for its time.. Physical fighting is not a condoned respect regarding the conduct of civil society.. Although, it says here that you were **not** under the influence of alcohol.. The man you struck with your fist was not harmed to an extent of using a hospital.. And he is .. As we can see.. He is a substantially larger and older man than you.. I would inform you that the man you punched.. Works for the parks department in this county and he has concluded to me that he does not worry about pressing any charges against you..”

The judge breaks momentarily while wrinkling the papers and shuffling them again and again.. Then candidly striking the microphone with brushing and crinkling noises.. Suddenly, the officer sneezes hard and then.. turns and coughs towards the window of the courtroom and blurts apologetic murmurs just before facing the room again.. The judge continues ..

“Mr. Brian have you ever played baseball before?” -Judge

“Baseball?” asked Brian “Yeah, sure I played baseball before..” -Brian

“So, then Mr. Brian .. Would you say you know the rules of baseball?” The judge asks as he leans back in his chair and the big-inning to grin in the way a cringe of scorn can smile.

“Yes, I think I would say I know the rules well..” -Brian

“Do you think the rules of Baseball are fair?” -judge

“Baseball Rules? Fair? Judge .. Why are you asking me about baseball rules?”

The judge suddenly laughs and stands and then asks the officer near the window if he heard him..

“Did you hear me ask him questions about baseball?” -judge

The officer coughs a bit and then squares up facing the judges side.. then the officer offsidedly states.. “Excuse me your honor.. and with all due respect.. but I do believe that you are asking him.. that.. um.. Some questions about baseball.. sir..” -officer

The judge begins laughing out loud and slumps back into his chair..

"Well folks .." blurts the judge . . "We are pitching a live game at these boys with every base.. what is it between a pretty girl and getting hit with a pitch? Should I call for a new ball?"

The judge then raises his hands and exclaims..

"I'll have to call this like the tie that hangs a runner.. Young Man.. You are dismissed.."

The Wifi Code

The morning spun past him as if the world wasn't even real anymore. Or perhaps it didn't matter to him anymore.. Sleepy slogs of water splashed through himself as he had gathered an extra bottle of water before he had found the Star's Church and he had plenty of refreshment as he awoke several times.. As he woke up again and again .. and turned back to his trump of restlessness.. And the cradle of fresh air had shaded his hopes of refreshing outreaches for reality.

And the day stirred around him as if it was his own.. as if the day was brightened by the ability to know.. That he had been with that day as a moment of compromise.. Contempt amongst the spiritual famine that troubled the breeze, as he became deep in a full breath of dwelling.. Like good rest does..

It may have been about 10 hours or so when he reached for more water to find that the second bottle of what was a little less than half full. The sky had calmed from a dry daylight.. Back to a contemplative perfection. Somewhere in the shade he imagined a fancy bath tub, but all he could see was a huge animal trough that had been sunk into the muddied ground.. And so strangely that it was more like a canoe that lost its stream.

Staggering back onto his feet, Brian stretched and even not believing that he had convinced himself to..

"Sheeesh.. man get up!" He shouts out as the voice of his yell seemed to record from the other side of sky's code of remorse for a steel heart.

Coughing and gagging dust.. He strolls off with the old bike and crosses back out to the highway and climbs into the ease of a squishy ride as he needed to find some more air for his tires. But, as he rode with no urgency.. A group of sparrows and other types of birds carried with him a sense of priority as he felt free from the traffic and the warmth from the pavement was even radiated as he could see a small stop farther than he could focus.

Brian found the stop wasn't even a gas station. Clanked the bike into a chain link fence and sat on the edge of a wooden porch area .. Moments later the door to the small store opened as a creaking spring strained.. into a woman's voice..

"If you need anything.. We are open." -store lady

Brian waves his hand up from a laziness and mutters softly as he was.. leaned back and staring at the sky.. "UMmmm.. Water please.."

The lady stalls for a moment and leans out the door a little further.. "OH.... ha.. yeah .. OK.. then I guess we have some water in the bathroom.. But.. um.. kid.. or who-ever.. we close in about an hour.."

The door slaps a typical screen door smack as the woman disappeared like a backstage exit..

The upside down view from where he was.. Was just about as beautiful as any birthright he ever couldn't imagine.. As if he planned it.. Thinking to himself of that.. Perhaps, he could plan a birth of social contraband. But his tongue was dry..

"Hey, kid are you ok?" the store lady standing over Brian asks him and nudges him to wake up.. "Do you still need some water?"

Brian sits up suddenly remembering that he meant to get up and get some water but he felt so relaxed and stretched out he had been in a trance by the ..

"I just don't want to make any sense.." He claims as he yawns and rubs his itchy dry eyes.. "I think I thought I did.. I think I was.. or.. Yeah.." Brian notices a man in a wheelchair sitting at the steps of the store porch.. An older man with a grin as silly as a hippie from woodstock..

"OH... ok.. He's alive" The hippie sounding man giggled up ..

"I um .. I think.. I was just trying not to .. makes sense.." -Brain appeared to ask as he reached for his backpack and pulled out one of the empty water bottles..

"Yeah, but are you going to survive.." -The store lady asks as she turns to the older man in the wheelchair..

"Hold on now..." The older man stops at her .. "So, kid.. What's your name?"

"Brian.." -Brian

"So, it's just a.. Brian.. Yeah, he does sound dry.. You better get you some water kid.." -old dude

The old dude in the wheelchair kinda chuckles in amusement.. "I thought you might be a dead ass washed up nobody.."

"Steve.. I gotta go .. Can you help this kid?" The store lady asks

Brian smiles tall as his humor can take him- "Washed uP? Naw I haven't showered in a week.."

"OMG.. go ahead and go Carolyn.." The Steve dude says.. "I think I will help him.."

Brian grins down at the older man as the dude leans back into the back wheels of his chair and balancing on 2 wheels..

"As is.. if cheap circus tricks war worth every penny.. I'm Steve.. And so that's your bike?" -Steve asks

"Well yeah.. I guess it is.." -Brian answers

"What do you mean .. You guess?".. Steve asks .. "That's how you got here Right?"

Brian spaces off stairing back over at the bike that had been half standing and stuck in the chain link fence.. as a curious angle..

"Oh, yeah.." -answers Brian "So it is.. How I got.. here.."

"OK.. double OMG.. kid.." Steve worries "Now, I think .. you really do need some water.. My place is a couple blocks.. if you want.. I got a shower.. But, I don't mean it as a weird thing .. I ain't gay.. You aren't qweer are Ya?"

Brian stutters back- "huh?"

"Just saying.. you look like you could use a shower and maybe some salt.." -says the Steve dude

"Salt?" -Brian asks

"Yeah, How many days have you been riding your bike?" -steve asks

Brian claims with a lethargic style of alert slag- "Like a week or something.."

"Just going nowhere? And you been drinking water and what else have you eating?" -asks steve

"I might have stolen some beef jerky a couple times.." -Brian admits

"Well, you need a hell of a lot more salt than a couple of pieces of beef jerky if you are riding and sweating like that.. So much.. Maybe a couple of days you might be ok.. but where are you going? How long are you going to be grinding down the highway?" -Steve corrects him

"I really didn't plan it.. I just decided to.. to ride away.. but, I think I feel it.. what you mean.. I guess I feel like I need some salt but.. . is that the same as a pizza craving?" -Brian

"But what kid? I know .. That's how traveling makes people sick.. And you are pedaling across the country land.. on a bike.. Just saying.. I ain't running a dog wash.. for ya kid.. I ain't gay.. I seen it.. But I know how kid.. travelers get sick from it.."

"From it?" -Brian repeats back like a deep blue something or other..

"Not enough salt kid .. Are you listening? Not enough salt!" -Steve shakes his head

Brian recollects the offer- "Right .. I mean.. Yeah, I ain't qweer man.."

"I've traveled and met many travelers.. You need salt, kid.. You need it.. " -steve

"So.. Why you in a wheelchair?" -Brian asks

"It's just for looks.. I can walk.." -steve warns

"Ah ha.. Well, how old are you anyway?" -Brian

Steve grins like that woodstock hippie again.. "I'm 68, but what does it matter? You know.. I live like I'm young .."

Brian reponds- "Yeah, well I thought you were younger than that.."

Steve slaps his knee.. "It's all in the salt, kid.. This society isn't prepared for what they know.. ya know?"

"Society is an excuse machine.." -Brian

"Yeah and that.. but you know what would be so funny to most people you will meet?" -steve asks

"huh?" -Brian

"They don't care, is what you will find.. and that's what.. so, funny huh?" -Steve reprimands..

"They don't care.. That's what's so funny?" -Brian stranges out..

Steve compromises.. "Yeah, that's what I always think is so funny.. You gotta have half a mind to hang out with one.. Everything else is a crossfire of the wrong way.."

Brian settles for the contentions .. "Yeah, I think I thought that was the case .. or something.."

"WTF.. Though.. How old are you?" -Steve inquires

"19.." -Brian

"You finished high school?" -Steve

"Um, not really but yeah.. I got my GED after dropping out the first year of highschool.. I guess I'm not into the scene of highschool.. I've been working as a paperboy.. But, I quit last year and then I just took the GED test this last fall.. I would've been in my last year of Highschool.."

"So, you just don't care or why did you decide to ditch it all? Girl problems? What's going on?" -Steve

"Well I didn't actually have a girlfriend but ..I think I do.. Or I have.. had.. or maybe I had some.. girl problems.." -Brian

"HA hA AH ha!! What the hell .. Maybe? you're not sure.. Then you must have.." -steve

"I think I just ain't as popular and all that.. as others who have social connections so.. I don't know how things are supposed to be.." -Brian assumes

"Times are changing.. but one thing is sure.. You can't change other people.." -steve

"Yeah, but I might sound weird, but I guess I realized that.. And the girls my age are having a lot more sex than I realized.. Especially the last 2 years of highschool.. but I had dropped out the first year of highschool .. so I haven't been around the others.. or anybody.. Very much .. But I hooked up with like 3 chicks so far.. before highschool.. but that was mostly before I dropped out.. But then a year later after I met this girl.."

"Oh.. Yeah, what's her name?" -asked the steve

"What the hell does it matter? If her fucking magic worked right I wouldn't remember.. Right?" -Brian questions

Steve laughs- "Oh .. So that's why that happens.." -Steve

"Yeah, so I met her when she was like 15 and I was almost 18.. And it all started with a backrub that turned into her inviting me over to bone and.. She had only hooked up with one other dude or something.. But I wasn't all that worried about it.. cause I was such a nobody.." -Brian

"Worried about what? Having a girlfriend?" -steve

"Yeah, I wasn't worried about having a serious girlfriend. or not.. So, we hooked up and then I didn't see her much after that.. She didn't try to find me.. Until about a year later after I dropped out of highschool and all that.." -Brian

"Oh, yeah ok. So she was pregnant?" -steve

"What? Pregnant? Naw.. not that I know of.. or not by me.." -Brian

"And so then she was working at some burger place or something and I was going to hook up with her.. But then .. She was talking about all these different dudes she'd met since she met me.. And then she said that she wanted to get fucked by 2 dudes at the same time and she wanted to see if I would help her with her fantasy.. But I was hardly thinking she must've been joking at any interest.. and I think she actually has 3 boyfriends or something.. like dudes that are older than me.."

Steve rolls out of his wheelchair laughing.. "What a slut!"

"Then I started riding around other places and looking around town and I realized that the girls my age are really getting around.. Way more than I imagined.. I guess that's not exactly my problem.."

"Lots of sex and that's not your problems.." -steve laughs harder

"Well. then it was also that most of her boyfriends were even older than me .." -Brian

"Ohhhhhh.. ha ha" Steve laughs in a fake style.. "Small world out there for some people.."

"I guess I just lost interest in hanging around. Because most of the other dudes were trying to get as much pussy as they could before the other chicks their age met older dudes.. Then that was a weird thing to realize.. Kinda cause I think people say towns like that.. They are called.. "truck stop towns.."

"TRUCK STOP TOWNS... Sheeesh.. these girls are the heartland's pride and joy.. I think I would.. Hear what you're talking about.. And so these towns are where the truck stop is the town's main event.. " -steve

"Exactly, And.. Well, then it was that she was asking me if I thought she should get birth control pills.. And I really didn't know why she would be asking me about it.. As if I was the only dude she could talk to about it or something.. I thought that I wouldn't be taking birth control pills if I was a chic. I would think it was an odd invention.."

"So, she wasn't your girlfriend?" -Steve

"Well I hooked up with her.. but.. No, she wasn't acting like a girlfriend to me.. but it was like she thought all the dudes that would talk to her. War all her boyfriends'.. And she would keep her conversation with me as if her conversations with other dudes and me were all the same person..or something.." -Brian cringes like a screaming tree..

"Freaky man!" -Steve screeches..

Brain continues- "Like a negative blame of denial personality or something.. and then I noticed that many people seemed to be like that.. Even the more I thought of it.. Or that I noticed.. How she was talking at me.. like that.. too.. but then.. What was weird about it was how they all seemed to be .. like a confidence struggle.. like socially.. It was like a power thing or something.. I don't know if it's just me or I think I see something and I just have nothing.."

"So, she asked you about birth control pills and what did you say?" -steve asks

"Maybe, I didn't know what I should say.. but I wasn't thinking about birth control pills being my problem.. But then I realized that if I date a girl that is using them.. then I'm that type of problem.. We only fucked like twice and then I didn't see her again for like over a year .." -Brian

"So, you hooked up with this chick a couple times after a back rub incident.. and then you didn't see her again for like a year ..and then she's wanting to bang you with another dude.. and has a birth control method plan like a red light district... Must've been a great back rub.." -Steve

"I guess I really decided that I didn't think.. Or I mean that I thought I wouldn't meet a chick that would need to ask me questions about birth control pills.. I wasn't prepared for her to ask me and then I thought that.. it wasn't my problem.. If I was a chic I would've never think of needing to do birth control pills.." -Brian tends "It just seemed like an extension of faith that I couldn't like.."

"So you think she was choosing something that you wouldn't and you think that and you aren't trying to live in the epitome of a sex pistol?" -Steve

"Yeah.. But I liked her.. I thought she was being dumb.. Because I realized that I hadn't been having lots of sex like that.. Like the way the girls war fucking around so much.. And so I noticed girls around town also had an uncanny way of acting strangely clueless.. it was weird.. because if I actually had a girlfriend I wouldn't expect her to be on birth control pills.. And.. but I never really ever had a girlfriend.. I only hooked up with a couple girls so far.. They didn't want to be my girlfriend or anything.. That other chick wasn't even my girlfriend though.. And I was sure I wouldn't need to ask my girlfriend about birth control pills.. I mean, how many people do you want to be having sex with? If I had a girlfriend I wouldn't imagine to be having sex with lots of other people very often.. So, in retrospect I think that we have those birth control pill products that were mostly what

I didn't agree with.. and other people do it.. Like what you said man.."

"Like what I said?" -asks Steve

"Yeah.. They don't care.. Like it's a power thing.. to not care.. or be foul or something.." -Brian cringes

"Kreepy cracker box!! Kreeps man! !" -Steve jumps up

"I didn't make birth control pills.. that's not my problem.. Fucking smart ass rich people.. serving society as a drunk moron.." Brian cusses around "My bright future as a bartender that doesn't get it.."

"You're only 19 right? you aren't not even old enough to be a bartender.." -steve

"Yeah, but I thought about it and I don't get this alcohol bullshit .. I think it's really pissing me off.." -Brian scoffs and shuvz at the conversation..

"So, bartending is out the window.." -Steve

"I guess I just kept riding around and realizing the town was a scumbag and then I quit my paper route and then I figured if .. Scumbags the case .. then the rest of the towns are just as bad and I could really get a great laugh! Looking around and making fun of people that are homeless as they insist to never talk about it.." Brain laughs..

"So scumbag is the case?" -says steve laughing too

"That is what is so funny .. I think.. Maybe some day.. I'll graduate into getting into a real fight against a real bartender.." -Brian trolls like iron maiden on vacation..

"What's that gunna prove?" Steves quicks back..

"I guess it doesn't matter if it proves anything.. I just don't like them and I'm not that.." -Brian

"That what?" -Steve

"I'm not that nice guy.." -Brian

"You aren't that nice guy?" -Steve

"Yeah.. you know.. That nice bartender guy.. that's everybodies' friends' or something.. giggled up about stupid ass drinks that don't help anybody with anything and such.." -Brian

Steve spins his chair and starts rolling towards the cross street..

"Well OK.. Well, if you're coming then.. Come on then.." -Steve

The Truck Fight

"Hey Brian!" Steve shouts from the other side of the bathroom door..

"I'm making some potato-mac.. " -Steve

"Potato-mac?" -Brian

"Yeah, it's instant Potatoes and macaroni and cheese.. mixed together.. I'm adding some salt to it.. a little extra bit.. Seasoning salts.." -Steve

Brian answeres as he gets into the shower.. "Sure whatever! I mostly lived as a frozen corn dog.."

"What?" -Steve

"That's what I usually eat.. but I eat anything I guess.." -Brian

"Well, I can add lots of salt to the potato mac and it's a smooth transition.." -steve

"Smooth transition?" -Brian

"You know .. Digestion and all that.. You need a medium to go with the salt.." -Steve

"A medium? Like a fortune teller?" -Brian asks

"ohhh.. yeah ok.. But it's a handle.. something to grip it with.. In your gut kid.. Like broccoli is a great salt medium broiled or whatever.. But you only want fresh veggies.. Not any stale stuff.. So I just quick up .. with the dry mix type things in hot water and stuff.."

The water in the shower sprays a loud splash as Brian shouts up.. "Sounds awesome! Man!"..

And in the edge of sanity paradise lost was found as some citizen kingship that may be a thing. When paradise is lost in the type-o-negative of the draw. What can be seen as luck and for others? They stretch 2 toed behind the wet sprockets keeping the conversation real and those other people know when your ends are spent..

Brian scruggles out of the bathroom door into the living space..

Steve strikes up quickly- "So I bought this old piece of property that was only this large garage building that was a workshop .. And the house for the property was sold to some other folks and they still live there.. on the other side of the field.." Steve invites as Brian huddles out from the doorway of the bathroom.. "Small Places and Small prices.. And then they built another garage next to the house.. But I still got a yard and stuff like that.."

"Yeah.. it's like a whatever it is, they call.. A rambler?" -Brian

"Yeah, right.. It was a 2 car garage and I added the tile sauna room as the bathroom on that end.. and I like it.. I reused the natural water spigot that was already in the ground on that side and I didn't need a kitchen but I eventually pieced together these cabinets from some scraps that looked cool.." -steve

"Looks cool.." -Brian

Added the A-frame ceiling and all that .. I put a loft bed up there that I let my visitors use, but if you're wanting to crash on the floor, I don't mind all that.. And actually I got a bunches of extra sleeping bags and coats or whatever.. if you want to take something for extra.. I don't know what you expect you're going to do and all.. But I got a bunch of extras from past adventures if you need a sleeper or any extra jacket.."

"I um, ok maybe.. I don't know how I would carry anything else.." -Brian

"Have you ever built anything on a house or anything?" -Steve

"Nope, I lived in an apartment with my mom.. And I guess I never have.. Built anything.. I do know how to fix my bike though.. I learned how to fix my bike for my paper route job.. But this bike.. I kindsa stole it I guess.. I left my paper route bike at my moms..”

“So you don’t want to go back?” -Steve

Brian shakes his head a little looking up and leaning back on the couch that was against the wall..

“I think I better not go back to that town.. and I think my mom is a weirdo..” -Brian

“Your mom is a weirdo? Hold on a minute and let me get this food handled..” Steve gets up from a recliner chair and spoons globs of potato mac into some bowls.. a couple of water glasses..

“This stuff might help a fortune teller..” -Steve concerned with humor..

“Yeah, I think I kinda decided that I need to be able to see the future.. I think I just noticed that like.. last year or something .. My mom wasn’t interesting to talk with and she wasn’t interested in me.. And she had no friends and she always watched TV as if it was her best friend.. And it was weird how I felt like I was interrupting her beautiful relationship with her TV..” -Brian

“What about your dad?” -Steve

“About the only thing my mom ever really told me.. That .. my dad said he was going to go into the Army.. but then she said that he didn’t.. And that’s all she said.. I mean.. um.. I asked her about it before but that’s all she ever told me.. And then she always gets pissed at me and tells me to shut-up if I bother her about anything..” -Brian

“So she doesn’t want to talk to you about anything and tells you to shut up.. Maybe you’re right.. OK then..” Steve nods in a confirmation.. “Maybe she’s a Weirdo huh?” -Steve asks in a humor

“It was like she despised my existence because of my dad or something else I just don’t know about..”

66

"Who? Your mom?" -Steve

"Yeah I guess I figured a ton of explanations of what might have happened but then I had to decide .. What does it matter? Knowing that.. it won't change that.. I'm a total complete nobody.. And my mom didn't miss my dad.." -Brian

"How do you know he didn't go into the Army or something?" -Steve

"What?" -Brian

"How do you know? She never told you what happened.." -Steve

"Oh, so you think that maybe.. he did go to the Army or something, but he never contacted her again?"

"Yo kid, i don't know .. Sounds like a mystery.. You can make assumptions, but.. Like you said.. it sounds like you will never know.. I'd say.. She was a weirdo man.. You lived with her and you feel like you don't know her very well.." -steve

Brian picks up the bowl and sniffs it up.. "ha.. smells cheesy! Here's to mom.." Brain says lifting the potato-mac up higher and says .. "And here is to never.. and I mean this.. I'm never going home.."

"To never going home then.." Steve claims "And god bless the lazy moms.. So what were you saying about Corndogs?"

"Hha?" Oh that's what I ate.. I mean.. What my mom got for me because.. that was cheap.. and she knew I had food as long as there was frozen corndogs in the freezer.. You know.. So, I told her that a couple years ago.. So she started keeping corn dogs in the fridge and I wouldn't have to talk to her.."

So, you been living on corndogs for the past um.. teen years.. And so you haven't actually talked with your mom for some um teen years.. even though you lived in an apartment together?"

"Yep.. And just for the record .. She spit in my face the last time I seen her.." -Brian

"Ouch! Man.. spit in your face.. that's harsh.. When was that?" -Steve

"That was about a month ago.. And I had been floating around town since then and I realized the whole thing about truck towns and that.. I was living in a trucker town of drugs and weird trailer parks mixed to look like a real town, but it was just a bunch of fake ass people.. Surrounded by a task force of lazy jerks that grew up on farms.." -Brian

"So, that's a good lesson?" -Steve

"Yeah, But the only other good people in town war retired military families but they aren't great for conversations.. But I was glad it was that simple.. I mean if she didn't want to talk.. Corndogs really are good.."

"Ohhh yeah, easy money then.. We could take your story and promote lazy moms to choose corndogs. Everywhere.." -steve laughs

Brian laughs at the thought.. "Taughahahahat! Oh yeah for sure.. I think maybe that birth control pills must mean society is borderline qweer.. Whatever happened to self control? Can you call off-sides on a referee?"

"Off-sides on a referee? What referee?" -Steve

"Obviously the industry .. as if.. Calling it on myself is all its worth I guess.." -Brian

"Borderline kweer? Maybe I think I might agree.. What in the hack is borderline kweer?" -Steve

"Dumb things that don't make sense like school detention and stuff like that.." -Brian

"Borderline Kweer.. maybe it is a thing.. could be a thing.. like a thing.. Sounds like there should be more to it.." - Steve thinks up, pointing his spoon in the air..

"Yeah.. well then.. Birth control pills are borderline kweer.." -Brian

"Yeah that's the inspiration from it then .. HA! funny as shit then!" -Steve

"That other chic wanted me to come over and fuck her with another dude.. And I wasn't interested in it.." -Brian

"Maybe that's a Borderline Kweer?" -Steve

"I think that.. is a Borderline kweer-ish thing.." -Brian

Steve speaks up in between sloshes of potato-mac.. "Oh craziness man.. sounds like there could be many borderlines with everything in society.. I think I got an extra notepad.. Steve jumps up and in through the doorway to his bedroom and starts digging around some boxes.. "Yap! Found it.. I had a whole box of these notepads! I ordered from the internet.. A couple years ago.."

"Maybe, sex with a condom is Borderline too.." -Brian pauses

"Oh, they got me!" Steve Cries.. from his room.. "That's Borderline too! Are you sure?"

"Yeah, I think maybe they already got me too.." -Brian stares at the glass of water in front of him..

Steve slaps a couple notepads down on the table- "You can have 2 if you want.. I got some pens in this drawer over here.. let me see.." -steve

"But I don't know.. Prostitution is just kweer or a borderline?" -Brian asks

"OH yeah.. Lap dances for money.. that could be the borderline.. of paying for sex.. SOoo.. Well, if paying for a lap dance would be the border line.. then paying for sex is just kweer.." -Steve

"Yeah.. Right.. So.. then if paying for a lap dance is the Borderline.. I think that sounds right.. I never even seen a strip club before.. But I've seen it in movies and such.." -Brian

"There's a strip club farther that direction on the highway.. But you aren't 21.."

"I don't even have an ID card.. I left it at my moms'.." Brain cries

"Holy ghost it's a wild bandit!.. No ID card!.." -steve

Brian digs around in his backpack but then he finds his wallet.. "Oh damn.. Lucky.. I do have my wallet.. I thought it was at my moms.." Brian picks up one of the notepads and puts a pen with it into his bag..

"Maybe, society was hypnotized and I'm not?" -Brian

"Hey man..the way you think you're nobody seems to work.. did you're mom ever showed you any guns or anything like that.." -Steve

Brian looks up at steve.. "GUNS? Naw.. She never had a gun as far as I know.. I never seen a gun up close.." -Brian

Steve leans back into his chair .. "When I was your age I never touched a gun before.. But I wanted to shoot one.. Like.. any gun.. And I never talked about it much.. But I wanted to see what it's like to shoot guns.. But I lived in a group home.. ya know.. and I could never get access to a gun or .. I shouldn't be asking about guns.. But I knew that boys that grow up on farms know guns and I thought I should know.. I learned a lot about guns later on though.. I learned how to do drywall and plumbing and flooring and fixing anything on a house.. I thought working on house fixtures of any kind was really fascinating.. My straight path from the boys home that didn't require me to be a military man.. But I'm 6 foot 1 and that's a perfect size of monkey to fix peoples houses when they don't have the time.. But I did it before there was cell phones.. it was different.. Business for a self employed fix anything man.. today is a ruckus in comparison to then.. It's been over 15 years since I answered a business call.. I advertised in a local paper.. It was easy.. Gas was cheap and trucks were hard.."

"Any Kids?" -Brian

"Yeah, I have a daughter but she was born in Canada.. I 've never seen her.. And her mother is a traveler.. You know she was already from Canada.." -Steve

"How old is she?" -Brian

"She should be about 30 or something.. Her mother wrote to me about it when she was 9.." -Steve

"They never came around to say nothing?" -Brian

"That's life.. Unpredictable. Her mom was a very confident soul when I met her.. I haven't worried about it.. But you know what you should worry about is.. Young fuckers your age in the cities with guns.. And they do have guns in the cities .. A lot of people even your age have guns.. As a traveler you need to keep your eyes open.." -Steve

"I never even held a gun in my hand before.. I'm sure my mom didn't have one.." -Brian

"Well, It's not like the movies.. I've got my collection of pistols.. I could show ya a gun.. ya know.. just so ya know what it's like.. At least you need to know how they work.." -Steve insists as he gets up from the chair and back through the doorway to his room.. I'll show ya one of the cheapest 9 millimeters in the world.. Mostly due to its high volume of manufacturing.. Steve caw-motions from his room a moment and then re-apeeres.."

"This is a Beretta 9 mil.." Steve gestures the gun pointed up at the ceiling and then cranks the safety and drops the clip into his other hand.. And they are solid but there are so many in circulation.. They became less special.. type of cheap.."

"Ah ha .. Less special cheap.." - Brian leans forward as Steve holds the gun out in view like a school trophy of achievement..

"You even know what the phrase 9 mil means?" -steve asks

"No.. not exactly, but I think it's about the bullets.." -Brian

"It's a larger hand gun.. designed to be able to shoot with most hand sizes.. Mostly all the armed Forces train with it."

"The 9 millimeter is the choice for short range stopping power .. Smaller caliber bullets just whizzed right through people but it didn't stop them if they had momentum.. Handguns are tricky about stopping power.. And the hand grip.." - Steve sets the gun on the kitchen counter and then hands the empty magazine towards Brian to see.. "Check it out.."

Steve hands Brian a bullet and the empty clip as he reaches back over for the Beretta that he had set on the counter..

Brian holds the bullet up and eyeballs the bullet.. "That's a 9 mil slug.. HUH?"

The Beretta clanked and clacked as Steve checked the barrel for rounds and he spun the gun around as if a showman's personality.. "Let me see the clip?" - steve says

Brian hands him the clip and Steve slaps in the clip and spins the gun into his hand.. The gun is awkward for him but he grabs the weight of it like he realized something important.. Steve reaches and snatches the bullet from his other hand and walls back to the kitchen counter.. Letting Brian look at the Beretta..

"It's gotta have a certain kind of weight to it because when the bullet fires.. So that's what's tricky about making them.. Handguns .. I have met people who make guns.. but handguns aren't as easy as a rifle design in that sense.. Because of the kickback.. " -steve

"Yeah.. oh right.. I guess I see that.. Maybe.." Brian turns the gun around looking at it and then grips the grip with both hands like he has seen on TV.. Aiming the Beretta across the room..

"It's a heavier feeling than I thought it looked.." -Brian nods

"The clip is empty but if it was full of rounds .. That adds more weight and then the weight of the thing changes while you fire it.. you know.. As the bullets fly out.. the gun gets lighter.." - Steve reinerates - "So, having a little heavier gun like the Beretta has less effect of that happening.. But lighter guns like Glocks and such have more effect about the rounds in the weight of the gun and aim at target practice.."

"Oh yeah, I've heard of that.. Glock 9 mil.. That's a gun right?" -Brian asks, sounding extremely genuine and nieve..

Steve steps close and shows Brian how to lock the barrel and pull the clip.. "The safety for most handguns are all the same.. See that.. just a post slide mcjigger.."

"So, what exactly would happen when I don't have enough salt for too long?" Brian still staring at the gun gripped in a both handed aim..

"Well, your body can't use other things or play out bad stuff very well without extra salt to play it with.. If you don't get some extra salt mixed enough.. I am serious.. You could get sick.." -Steve

"POwW.." Brian says as he acts to have shot the gun in slow motion.." maybe ..ha .."

U.S. Social Security hotline # 1-800 772-1213 7am to 7pm Monday through friday.. S.S.D.I. didn't have a hotline because we didn't talk about it.... File'd as a happenstance..Social Security doesn't need an ID card for US citizens but all the grocery stores all want you to have a "STORE CARD" for all the grocery stores but that's not a bad clue about how we should have a social security picture ID card? Foul'd marketing as a socially mass'd happenstance ...

The Wifi Code

As Brian wakes up in slow motion and quickly realizes he needs to piss.. He jumps up while re-remembering which direction the bathroom was. Old Steve passed out and leaned back in the recliner.. Brian hits the shower back on.. And peeees one of the longer pisses of his life.. And another rinse with a lengthy hot shower..

He had washed his clothes in the washing machine and he needed to put them into the dryer.. So, he scamp'd back into the bathroom's chili air.. Looking for some soaps to rinse with.. A camping cooler was under the sink and surrounded by camping items and a packed tent.. Other jackets and such.. like Steve had said.. Brain bumped the cooler open reaching in to find an object in the bottom that had been wrapped in a T-shirt..

"Hey, is everything ok with ya?" -Steve asks, half asleep'd like a citizen fish standing at the bathroom door..

"Everything is alright I just had to piss and then I'm moving my clothes into the dryer.. I'm still rinsing off.." -Brian bumps the shower water back off..

Steve wanders back into his room..

Brain looks down at the object in his hand.. A wrapped up small object.. He unfolds the older t-shirt.. Brian reaches down under the sink again and into the old cooler and feels around.. His hand found some small box shaped items marked as .25 ACP bullets.. and a couple more t-shirts..

Brian finds a chrome like handgun wrapped up in the t-shirt and reads under the scopes of his breath.. "Raven Arms MADE

IN USA" He says as he stands to put his pants back on.. He quickly pulls the cooler out from under the sink and takes 3 boxes of the Bullets ... .25 ACP bullets.. and then Brian scamps back out from the bathroom as the sound of the dryer smooths the sense of mischief.. He sinks the small handgun and 3 boxes of bullets into his pack.. And exhaustedly considering a small shooting practice.. lag-wagon'd in thoughts of for-warning of the experiments'.."

Brian stays awake long enough for his sox and hoodie to be dry.. About 5 AM .. And after setting everything under the sink as if untouched.. He set out refreshed as the sun was coming up.. Like the way a nobody does.. With his handle and his shoes...

Space Age'd as a patch lure in the micro-soft'd systems coat-tails.. Reading like code chainz or maybe its that weed strain ..like how WE are seriously fucking cute.. A food fight that crash-indo's through clichae'd in-hu Windows.. And as the good book acts as the world wide coffee domination.. As if the Greed had a finish line.. Living like a bouncing soul in the Greek terms of survival are pretentious.. But they are still grinding and burning like that electralight.. With the Hackney and frost bites riding the radio waves three steps through the hot stone.. planning the electra-fight as a bumpy road flight..

And the definition of Human.. as a trafficking strategy.. is not a legal coincidence.. US? PLEASE DO knot prank call ..The National Human Trafficking Hotline # 1 (888) 373-7888 - 2021

Bad clues rhyme with bad news and you need some salt? "it" .. are some things about digestion and about how using food can be foolish.. Those differences are the indifferences between how an adult uses food and how a child uses food.. Public School didn't seem to notice.. if you war a nobody.. they war.. waiting for you to notice.. but you waited too long.. Hindsight experiments planned as anti-social tragedy .. if your parents didn't tell you

about those things about food by the time you're 12 years old..
You must be a nobody.. "lordosis".. Happenstance'd at you.. Tail-
bone'd is house-broke.. And or ask your self if you feel like an
"Emotional Urge Experiment" that aims to disorient a nobody..

AND THAT iS HOW THE SHIT LEARN'd HOW TO
FLY

The Truck Fight

Brian road ahead into the morning as a time kept scapegoat like the difference between an intern and a free hooker.. Superior in that explanation of free as a constant contrast of about how things don't last and an endless question about any fedderer'd contentions. Just stay with the picture as it leans for swinging utters.. Leaning towards impressions that some may assume .. that some may have more time.. More time than others? Guessing around the history while the sultry past is rev-ha-lay-shun..

Learning how the past and the future will always reflect a mirror of infatuation.. At least if you have time for that.. Worrying about superiority as a realization of the millencolin..

In anti-space, yours doesn't matter..

The future becomes that unconquered elite light sugarcult'd if you want to be more grounded.. Unidentified and undefined .. below the radar and powered as healthcare enthusiasm.. Billed to Obey.. The future has that ring of stereophonic cliche .. of 9/10th'$ of the law.. Between how she needs a fight.. to get a house .. but she wants it.. Then the cards waterfall like call-oh-kneeds.. And then I thought of her .. Asking if the knowledge could've been looking for a reason to double back-slash in that fairy tale .. It was as if a body bribe was an Emergency.. Marketed as anti-self insinuations.. Which would mean.. that the marketing bots could be learning reboot.. but they still got lag.. Trying to remember which is as hard as referencing a book of keys.. I must've forgotten about how they created lag.. So she might get slugged but she thinked, hymn later.. maybe.. Whichever version the program suggested war all worth freelance wages.. piloted through the general public's pocket books.. Because it's a real happenstance..

And because to some people.. Getting tired meant you earned your hubcaps..

Brian air'd up and refilled water through the day as the road was never ending and the view dimmed into an afternoon. And in-between the intersections of power in numbers and less is more. Compromising how living as a novelty activity can be an excuse to compromise.. He exited the highway roads after seeing a sign for a camping spot.. Invisible as a blind possibility.. A parking area of sand and dirt clues a petty place to hang out with evidence of many sites .. The roadside embankment trail'd into the woods under a bridge that crosses a river.. Brian coasts into a slow and follows a trail that banks on towards the river.. The river was high and perfect.. As if finding the right place is supposed to be worth it.. Brain carried the bike into some bushy trees and it fell perfectly into a branched style tree stand. The site at the river bed was well used and a fresh blackness in the fire pit area of recent use was as if somebody had been there within a week.. At least or so..

Beer cans showed evidence'd of morons in the area..

As a nap insue'd upon the clash of no-fx..

The Wifi Code

Brian wakes suddenly as a stirring noise abruptly pops.. and again and again.. The sounds of a vehicle parked nearby as he looked up to see the daylight was still.. The banging sounds of somebody smacking or banging the side of a vehicle is what it sounded like.. after it putted'd and seemed to stop running in a creative way..

"Popcorn!" a voice yells.. as another hard bang and the truck door slams..

A short older dude and a gutter pup kid that could have been a hillbilly straggle from the trail as Brian was still laying near some trees and the bike..

"Looks like we got some catfish.." -The older dude says to the river kid..

"Don't wake me up.. I'm just half dead and wondering.. You dudes fishing here?" -Brian

"Actually no.." the kid said.. "We be barbecue'n.. Are you fishing?" -river kid asks

"If studying the back of my eyelids is fishing then I'm an mvp player this year.." Brian laughs "Fishing is a novelty with no competition.. very intense and the rewards are either unbelievable and or don't amount to much in return.. Naw, I don't fish.. but I have.." Brain cackles..

"How the heck? Did you ride a bike out here?" -The river kid questions

"Yeah, I been riding for a week or something.." -Brian

"You been riding for a week? Where you going?" -River Kid

"I don't know.." -Brian

Both them laugh about Brian .. "Well bro.. Looking thin man.. did you get caught in a dis-tatefull humor match of some strangeness?" -asks the older dude..

Brian laughs back again- "What does that have to do with looking thin? I'm just studying about how to be a stranger.. And or how they survive.. you know .. as a leaf that fell from nowhere or something.."

"So this guy is that stranger type of shit then.. I have ever never seen.. Travelers beware.." -river kid

"When god shits on me.. I say it's that type of luck ..you can't fathom.." -The old man grumps..

"What? I thought that.. ALL LUCK is unfathomable.. that's how you know. If you can't explain it.. that's luck.." -Brian negates

"OH yeah ha ha yeah.. I think I might argue with that.. but I know I can't fathom a fancy enough retort to get it started.." -old man

I been eating some salty stuff but I got a couple a bloody noses from it yesterday.. I think maybe too much salt for riding the bike and stuff like this.. So I stole some hotdog buns and i been collecting the ketchup packets and mayonnaise and stuff like that.. -Brian sits up rubbing his neck and trying to wake up.. "And I keep getting this weird feeling in my ear.. and my jaw.." -Brian sits up more stretching and yawning..

The old man laughs up- "Be careful with that".. The old dude nods at the bike.. "If you're riding that thing on empty.. You could hurt yourself.. You don't want to break your bawh-heeerr..".. The older dude bends pointing to his lower back.. "I broke my bawer once.."

Brian looks up at them- "My baw-hheer? what the hell is a bawh-herr?"

The river kid and the older dude look at eachother and giggle.. "Well.. I think its your ass.. Yeah.. hows your back?" -asks the older dude..

"What?" asks Brian.. "My back? Why?" Brian stands up feeling lighter than usual and claims..

"OK.. so sometimes I have been getting a little light headed.." -Brian bends side to side like a rubber band as his neck cracks.. and then he asks again looking at his stomach .. "My baw-her?"

The river kid looks at the older dude with a grin "OK, I think I know I told you that sorry?

The old man grins back- "What sorry?"

"About how I got shined.." -The river kid

Both them look at brian giggling as Brian is still yawning with one finger wiggling in his ear like it itched or something.. and he asks candidly - "Have you guys herd of a game called scratch?"

The old dude laughs a moment and asks the river kid- "What did you get shined with?"

"The rich end of the cow pasture mixed like the sour side of a rag of muffin.." -River kid

The old dude looks up at the sky like he is remembering something and says.. "A rag of muffin?" then the old dude looks at Brian- "Have you been eating muffins?"

"I think maybe I'm urged for some reality.. but.. muffins haven't been on my menu.." -Brian says as he keeps stretching and reaches into his backpack for a water bottle.. "I had a dream about blueberries though. And then my story dropped out of school and I decided I didn't fit in.." Brian gulps some water.. "Here I am.."

The river kid talks more- "it was the other dudes girlfriends' .. is why I left school.."

Brian kaws up..- "Haw ha ha.. Other DUDEs' girls' friends'?"

"Yeah.. these others' dudes' girlfriends'.." The river kid laughs .. "And they are everywhere.."

"You dropped out of school because of some other dude's' girlfriends'?" -Brian asks

"Well, mostly because they wanted to control my thoughts.. but that's just my wicked paranoia .. about things.. that even if I could prove it.. I still ain't got nothing.. but neither of us are going home.. And you know why.." -river kid

"I know why? I think I'm as home as it gets for a poor nobody.. I'm trying to think its an advantage against the credit bureaus as a floater that avoids getting flushed.." -Brian

The river kid cowards as he throws some small rocks at trees across the river..- "We aren't supposed to be here.. And I mean outside.. Many people been fallen to the .. to those ideas.. Ideas that they will get home.. I can hear them but I can't hear myself enough to save the day.."

"Fallen ..about thinking of home?" -Brian

"Yeah .. They believe that they will get home and that there will be somewhere to call home.. but that's a huge mistake is what I realized.. Because that's a nieve objective.. I forgot about home.. You better than to know .. home is outta the ballpark .." -The river kid tosses a rock up and catches it.. "And we are living in it.."

"Living in it? I want to be beyond it all.." -Brian

We live in a ballpark .. The ballpark.. The Ballpark.. and we aren't supposed to.. You know.." The kid laughs.. "We aren't supposed to sleep inside the ballpark.. downtown.."- The river kid laughs more.. "And you can get in big trouble for sneaking into the ballpark downtown at night.."

Brian kackles.. "OK ..that sounds like it.. That must be one of those rules they set against ya in that game of scratch that they tender.."

The old man pipes up- "And you better not be sitting around the streets too long.. or anywhere too long.. you're not supposed to be here.. man if I could give you the best advice.. don't trust nobody and stay invisible.. Nobody can lie and cheat and steal like poor people.. they can lie about anything.. but rich people don't.." The older dude laughs "See that.. Rich people.. They lie about nothing.." -The old man laughs hard more..

"Well I think that I really don't trust nobody.. Ha ..I think .. Not even myself.. Reality is so harsh'd.. I guess I need to know how to hack my brains.. in case that it may have already been bush-whacked.. I must have decided that's how I keep the truth safe from realities' claws or whatever the game is.." -Brian stutters.. "I say bring em on.."

"I think that I figured I would have some friends. You know.. Way back in 3rd grade I looked at the 6th graders and I thought.. someday I will have friends and move on.." -river kid

The old man starts vigorously laughing and coughing up a lung.. "Still waiting.. HA! Yeah, so what happened in 4th grade?" The old man coughs..

Then the bubbly old dude grins and smiles at Brian..

"Well you don't have too.." the old man keeps laughing at Brian.. "like gay people!" The man laughs hard and gasps for breath.. "oh man.. I am heartstruck!" and the old man fakes a heart attack dramatically.. then falling to the ground.. "All this lord has got.. is a hurt ass!.. some things mean kaw-boo-goal and other things mean kaw-boggle.."

Brian smiles at the man's humor as if he had a friend.. "I ain't too sure about the Kaw booogle.. but the Kaw-boggle is sounding ok.." -Brian

"Well .. I think in a bigger city that means you are actually less important.." -River kid

"Oh yeah.. I think I thought that was a consideration.. This may sound strangely ironic.. but I think I do want to live around a place where I'm.. just a number.. But I don't know if that means

I want to fit in.. So being a real nobody is knowing that I'm still nobody anywhere.. but, I can still choose where I like to be.."

"Explains how you got here.." the old man wrestles with some items and begins setting up a grill.. "I'm making pancakes.. Barbecue style.. You want some barbecue pancakes?"

Brian looks up at the old dude.. "Barbecue pancakes?"

"Yeah and we got fresh blackberries.. We been picking them all week.." -the river kid says

Brian turns towards the river kid "Barbecue pancakes and blackberries? SOoo.. OK.. I think that I might need to taste this.. Since I'm learning the techniques of the squatters paradise.. I think in contrary of that.. We must be leaving.. or leaving for home or something.. But not getting there is the funny part?"

"Yeah ah ha.. see I know that even sounds good.. Barbecue pancakes and blackberries has a ring of comfort that could be as cool as any ice cream.. but I still never made ice cream before.." -the old dude says while continuing to prepare the grill .. "the only things that are advertised as real are dairy products.. And what's that sound like?" -the old dude laughs

"Dare-he products?" -asks Brian listening..

"Nothings been so real.. They can't agree on what a milkshake is supposed to sound like.." The river kid laughs - "Because they didn't want to admit that they made one.." -followed with more laughter

"Dare-he Products?" -asks Brian again and laughing

Old dude- "Well after what I think I know.. I seen it.. If there is any game that I can show for.. its a game that is based from a stupid ass sound about how my mom poops me out.. Like a joke about the bartenders that aren't allowed to shit sitting down.." the older dude then farts and laughs more.. "Whatever a game could be about I wonder.."

"What? When ? how? What.. Bartenders aren't allowed to shit sitting down?" -asks Brian

"Naw, that's not a real game.." -Says the river kid

"Because .. I told you already.. my mom poops me out .. that's why.." -the old dude answers..

I thought you said that the game was about how.. if it makes more than one dude.. then that means the food won.. -River kid

"OH yeah.. that was part of it.. But its all started from.. .about how my mom poops me out.." -old dude

"Yeah alright ..That's one of those heard .. truths.. that also seems too much.. Even from the creator's mouth.. himself.." -Brian

The old dude jokes back.. "OK then.. I've said too much.. And it's too much for your human fathoms.. So that's why I say that all I need to say is that.. My mom just poops me out. And that's my good enough answer for anything.." -The older dude grins and starts putting the coals in the grill.. "I don't think I know why the game is messed up.. but it doesn't make sense if you think about it.. but they say it doesn't make sense if you have more than one.. so then the food won.. But I think I can't remember if that's how they hid reality from the life.. or if that's how.. He.. is living.." The old dude looks up at the sky and wonders..".. became a secret.. And then it's just like the manual said and how the long division as algebraic circumferences weren't enough to know the truth as an indifferent from any other time.. and then if that's the game .. as far as I know.. what does that say about me? and my survival.. I think at the end of the answer .. you will always get the square root of a charley horse.."

The river kid laughs- "oh yeah.. I felt it.. but I didn't get it.. and you heard it right hear folks.. And on the day that you eat of it.. you will be like god.." -river kid

"So I traded a milkshake for a fair shake? When did I do this deal?" -Brain asks as he is leaning back against a tree..

"You're not doing it son.. it is doing you.." -The river kid laughs

Brian laughs back .. "I'd say .. Con'd-a-sin-ding.. as explaining moral licensing with interjections of subversive anti-value.."

the river kid jumps from climbing a tree.. "No cigar man.. I know why.. The game is owned.. but it isn't by nobody and it isn't somebody either.."

Brian looks over at the river kid.. "the game is owned? What? Seriously.. tell the US who this game-master is.."

"Nature owns the game.. And it's unfathomable how that works.. For you as a human person. But I can tell you something about.. it.. Nature and ownership.. That your mortal minds can try to understand.. Nothing owns Nature.." -old dude

"Nothing owns Nature? God doesn't own Nature?" -Brian

"Nope .. That's what I realized.. You know.. God doesn't even own Nature.. And nature doesn't want anything.. it's purely selfless.." -old dude

"Nature doesn't want anything?" -Brian

"Nature always wins because nature makes more sense .. And it doesn't want anything.." -old dude

"Nature makes more sense? And it doesn't want anything?" -Brian asks

"Yeah right.. that was it.. and then ..the game hurts god.. But the game can't hurt Nature.. And God doesn't make sense.. god is stupid ass crazy because god wants.. Ya know.. Nature is real and God is a phantom of human needs.. because God made man... And nature is God's purest creation because God isn't nature.. God is human and that God wants and needs and is supposed to play with nature but nobody can control Nature.. Not even God. " -old dude

"Nature always wins? So this is the explanation that doesn't make sins?" -Brian

"Man is the seed of god.. the seed of her nature.. But he lives as that defiance of nature.. You know.. of her.. She is that Nature.. as hymn.." -river kid

"The Nature of God? God is a sexist creature.." -Brian

"A cop told me that .. And when I was complaining in line at the store.. He said that I can't afford to complain and that I was too small to be the hero.. And he said.. So you better go hide in a hole and prey to god.. " -The river kid laughs "You know what though? .. the next day I seen a chick at school that I always want to talk to .. but I mostly have a problem with thinking of anything clever to say.. But I told her that .. Ya know.. What that cop told me.. and she laughed and about a week later she asked me to come study with her .. and I got laid.." -river kid

"What naw.. No way.. What happened?" -Brian

Well I couldn't believe it.. She drove me from school to her place.. To her house .. and we got there and nobody else was home.. I was hella into her and I'm sure she could tell.. and then I was in the kitchen getting a glass of water and she went to the bathroom.. But then it was like 10 minutes or so and I was like.. What the hell.. and I started getting the stuff out of my backpack and then.. Suddenly, there she was.." -river kid

"There she was?" -Brian

"I mean.. There she was.. She looked at her wrist and said that we had about an hour and told me what was what.. AND.. She was walking across the kitchen in some panties and a skinny t-shirt.. and soaked from hot shower water... When she said it.. I couldn't think of arguing or thinking of much anything else to talk about at that moment.." -The river kid said

"Did she start cooking some grilled cheese sandwiches?" -Brian laughs

"Her hair and everything was all soaked and she was still steaming from the hot shower like a crazy wet t-shirt fantasy or something.. " -river kid

"Oh.. praise the angel of joy.." -Brian

"Yo man this chick was so smart.. And she had a nerdy collection of condoms.. I probably would have fallen in love.." -River kid

"I think that I would have.. so you married her?" -Brian

"Naw.. But she made me get in the shower with her and she didn't want to me to make any sounds and she kept acting like a sextress boss bitch.. it was surreal.. but I couldn't complain.. I couldn't believe it.. how she was .. and I never seen her act like that way.. at school or anything.. it was like unreal.." -river kid

"highschool?" -Brian

"It was the last year of highschool.. So she went off to a nice college.. Ya know.. I haven't seen her since highschool.. it's been a few years now.. -river kid

"Good one.. You only studied with her once?" -Brian

"Naw we studied about 5 times or something like that.. but she always made me get lost as soon as it was over.. But that always seemed so funny to me every time.. And she told me not to talk about it.. But she didn't have a boyfriend at school that I knew of.. So, I didn't feel too strange about it when I would see her at school.." -river kid

"Sounds like you got bossed .. but you funny boned her.. a string of day-dreams later .. and then highschool was over .. and then you never seen her again.. Maybe that's some real luck?"

"If luck was a feeling.. I must have had it.. a few times between 3:30 and 4:30.. in 1999" -river kid

"Well I know what it rhymed with.. if you want to make a song about it.." -Brian

"I think I heard it already.. on the radio.. A story about how my time happened to me.. And I was inundated.." -River kid

The older dude is clanking things around to light the grill up..

"OK, so I could tell you this.. about how nothing.. works.. and how nothing happens.. but it doesn't make sense.. And you kids always get mad at me when I tell you about this magic trick.. When after you poop .. and then you drink some water and you feel like you're done.. And timed out and then some time goes by and then you get a surprise with a magic poop.. So then if you want to stop nothing from happening then.. How are you going to stop nothing from happening? You kids need to learn how to accentuate.. Don't you like magic?" -the old dude gas laughs like a sideshow.. Good thing you guys are so stupid or I'd never get around to my chest exercises.." -the old dude blurts as he lights a ciggerrette.. Because nothing is a huge butt pirate.. Unless we can afford our own cigarettes.. at any rate as affordable butthole surfers can be .. there is a difference in luck and how magic works as luck or as nothing and whatever.." -old dude laughs even harder.. As he flares a torch into the barbecue and it bursts up into fueled coals fired bursts of heat and fumes.. "Good luck on keeping track of it.." The old dude says and continues muddering about over the smoking barbecue and chuckling.. "And I think that I could share some insight on an important lesson about camping .. Don't feed blackbirds barbecued onions.."

The river kid points at the old man.. "No I get it.. God doesn't make sense.." -river kid

"So then.. nature can't fathom it.." -Brian ads

"Black jack! baby!" -The river kid shouts

"Blackjack?" -Brian

"Nature can't even fathom it.. SO.. I must be nature.." -river kid

"What type of catch 22 is this?" -Brian

"its a catch 33.. add eleven and multiply nothing divided by pure bullshit.." -river kid

"OK.. this is something I think I was noticing the.. Humerology happens'd.." -Brian insights

"Yeah.. well catch 22's are only useful if you got a better explanation for selflessness.." -river kid points

"Multiples of eleven? So what the hell is .. a catch 33 exactly?" -Brian

"Some type a double negative with a broken space bar that catches all the real big fish.." -river kid

The old dude laughs hard from the grill with a cup in his hand and mixing the pancake mix.. "Nobody really wants to know what the good life feels like.. Now does that sound right?" -old dude rants on..

"All the white people's church services I've ever been to always sound intentionally bad and boring like I got stuck in a Barney episode.. So, what's the good life supposed to feel like? Asinine without a cause.. Jesus is a clown and God is an excuse to survive.. then a blah blah blah blah through the cycles of filling the void and the urge of social status'.. I know what it tastes like.. finding normal is the secret.. but Barney ain't no normal dinosaur and I fart more normal then any Barney episode could strive to be.. I'll tell ya something about magic though .. All magic is restricted to time.. And the best magic takes the best of your time.. All the magic that purple dinosaurs ever know'd is peanut butter jelly time.."

"it's like sometimes .. I think some people really are against rock and roll.. but what else would you compare them too?" -Brian

"And that's why hip hop had to happen.." -river kid

"Then.. So hip hop is rock and roll?" -Brian

"What isn't rock and roll?" -the old dude scratches back

"HUm? Well plenty of things.." Brian grins.. "like Mr Roger's neighborhood ain't no damn rock and roll.."

"Yeah but ..what about the things in life that are supposed to be rock and roll'n.. but then you find that they aren't rock'n.. or rolling.. " -old dude

"What? what do you mean?" -Brian

"You know.. the other people with all the time in the world.." -river kid

"All the time in the world? What the hell are you talking about? that sounds like a lot of time to be dealing with.. All the time in the world.. too much time for me to worry about.." -Brian

"OK! Exactly! how the hell would you keep track of all the time in the world?" -river kid

"I might build an Army just to protect myself from the math tests it would make me do .. tracking all the time in the world.. But I think they made different time zones in order to keep track of that.. and one of them was that green-witch.. you know.. London time zone.." -Brian

"Green-witch? Oh yeah.. Are you sure? I thought that .. I think I remembered.. it was green-rich.." -old dude says.. "At any rate.. I think I don't want to keep track of it all.. Everyday.."

"Green-Rich?" -Says the river kid..

"Naw Man.. It's Greenwich .. And then remember the .. MEAN-time part.." -Brian

The old dude starts chuckling and dings the wooden spoon on the top of the grill.. "Oh ok I think I know that's a sign.. I remember it related to my past life as a schoolboy .. and a funny thing that at one point or another.. I wasn't allowed to talk about strawberries in school.." -old dude laughs more.. "And so spilling a beer was .. the party.. HA ah ha! foul? or it was that.. the party is a spilling beer .. as the foul at large.." ..

"Damn'n you .. you fishers of men.." -Brian cries with a fist in the air and laughs..

"I know there is a certain grade of knowing privacy.. If people cared about what she did when she was a teenager.. She probably wouldn't have taught me how to read.." -old dude

"So.. Privacy divided by bads and then multiplied.. hads.. with the humerology of a warlord.." -Brian contemplates alloweded'd..

"As a witness.. I think.. Here's to moving on.." -River kid spouts

"Moving on to what? the humerology of a warlord?" -Brian

"Well .. could nothing be that?" -River kid

"By the time you asked.. they already forgot where you found it.." -Brian

"Found what?" -River kid

"Pancakes are up!" -the old man shouts..

Socialized influence of people with self control issues seem to swing into cocaine use in similarly precocious ways... and not all exactly the same.. mark study..

"It's a vastly crazy insinuation to keep track of all the time in the wilded culture of the world .. and combined with the harlotry as covert'd segregation tactics.. that spins hymn into a hopeless romantic.. in the loss of her.. Does that mean we are sucking on the false considerations of the hypothesis of marketing wonders? Agreeeesive ... sounding tungs and hit-lure'd.. English just sounded more friendly.. in a recording and remembere'd from.. And people from France have... I would.. wasn't a stone.. but I might've rocked the boat.. It was concluded that.. sexy attitudes had a substantial influence on daily provisions and won the war'd.." -the old man scoffs..

"So.. why did they win?" -Brian

"Their ideas loved them more.." -Old dude

"Superiorized by an idea of potential power? -Brian

"Potential power is of magic.. by the inspiration of expectations.." -River kid

The old dude stews the conversation .. "Society is a lucky happenstance more so than not.. which side would god be on? the luck or the not?"

"Ok so wait a second.. Who won?" -Brian

"the idea of overcoming itself as what?" -old dude

"So maybe .. We won as a planned peace of lucky ass? thats a lesson?" -River kid

"AH ha! ha ha.. And an accident is just a step.. child.." -old dude

"So then we have the whole of the idea as it is overcoming itself?" -river kid

"Wow-we just redefined that reality.. Self worth is a daily attribute I can handle.. And.. I decided.. parents are over-rated.." -brian

"Yeah.. fuck the whole thing.. self sabotage'd on a mass equation.." -river kid

"I am that overcoming self.." -Brian states

"You are the overcoming self? What the hell does that mean?" -river kid

"The experience of the overcoming self.. theory in motion of our melancholic socialized charity.. You know what it means.. Better go to charge.. or your a battery.." -Brian laughs and repeats.. "You better go to charge or you're a battery.." LOLO Brian laughs.. as the river kid chuckles

"I know what the trick is ..and how it is something.. though.." -the old dude laughs.. "God needs to be lost .. And.. if she wasn't lost .. she wouldn't ever come.." -The old man bings the top of the grill with the wooden thing again and laughs..

Brian's eyebrows raise as he laughs with them.."Let me get this.... Ha.. SOoo.. God is a female .. and ..Nature doesn't want.. and then.. They hate to admit that I really need some sugar and she just needs to get lost.. that's the secret of society's definition for horrible?"

"That's God's recipe of most the unconditional tree huggers.." the old dude rattles on..

Brain winds up a comment .. "Trying to understand how society works.. is so ouch.. It's like learning to have a sense of humor in doggy style.." -Brian

"If you think that sound'd bad.. I was going to talk to my dogmatologist about it but I couldn't find hymn.. Must've got stuck up.. Ha ha.. That's God's ass.." The old dude laughed harder again as the laughing seemed to never stop.

The TRUCK FIGHT

And as the words of advice rained like instant gratification lifestyle on fool go.. And this bitter-fly-tec kicks like G-force with sex as more valuable as a weapon.. Ora-trigger-ometry when dealing with nerves that aren't supposed to be there.. Ora those nerves also'd suppose'd to remember how you got there to begin with.. Ecstasy butterflies like a knife in the heart because that's what they made it for. Even numbers of the population agree that sometimes the chords come across more like a limp bizkit..

Backed up.. means stuck and other mental restructuring that invites the Farm's oddities.. Growing is normal as arguing for blooming as magic..

As if the squares war the difference between the circles of fake and real..

I find myself with a stale fart that reminds me about a feeling in the edge of my foot.. And Marshal Law creates farthest fetch fashions.. Making sense of smoking seeds..

And some people think they are on the girls' side ..

And some people think they are on the boys' side ..

And some people think they need to pay US to make sense..

If the salt factory of the city could strangle a circus..

I need to center in my self purpose.. But when the shit hits the morning page like a wild rage on the subject of like..

Advertising like commando paper tune'd about a rebelling shithead..

You don't know what like is like.. you don't even know if like has had it..

You need hot water therapy the same as a machine shop needs a welder..

Said that.. being very tired and unrested was the driving force of social unrest.. Questions of cosmic wonders ask'd if the seed of God's nature wouldn't be to protect?

Although, Still wondering about dirty birds giving a shit.. I figure they think it's a holy thing to do..

Giving a shit and all that..

The Wifi Code

Brian leaned up strange'd and rolle'd over to notice he was woken from a cell door crashing on the cell next to him.. But it wasn't morning.. And that wasn't what time it was..

Remembering he was in a jail cell as the low light made it easy to see.. A voice of another cellmate echoes through the cracks of the ugly vent plastered with soap in a fancy toilet paper problem.. The click and clack of a cell door pops open and a sound of a tired morning begins.. livid as lifeless can be.. Brian sat up to see an older man limping across the bay and turning on the shower.. Another older dude peeks out into the bay and kicks the door several times before disappearing again .. followed by shouts and bangs as other dudes wake up.. Another door pops open as another younger dude swiftly strolls across the bay to gather the newspaper from the day before.. And the TV hanging from the wall announces the traffic updates and gardening tips.. Politics and local drama echo around the bay as Brian thinks about why and when he got arrested for trespassing.. Why war the cops hands shaking so bad.. maybe the nurse was complimenting a sense of severed limbs as the man in the shower insisted that they made his injury worse.. By insisting to put ice on it.. The dude reading the paper hops up telling the older dude to shut the fuck up and then tosses the newspaper into the air.. The younger dude starz jogging around the room and coughing and such as if.. Pounding his chest and making odd sounds like sexual problems do.. Suddenly he stops and squats in the best view of the camera and proceeds to drop a deuce.. The intercom buzzes with a female voice.. zzzz.. pfff..

"Are you pooping on the floor?" -jail guard

The young dude bounces back up laughing like a toy gun as a means of common humor.. He then walks over to the bay intercom button pushing the button over and over and over claiming candidly..

"There's poop on the floor... there's poop on the floor..there's poop on the floor.." -jail bird

The intercom buzzezz again.. "Lock-down right now.. lock down!"

The young dude makes his way back to his cell and imitates a train.. "Choo choo choo choo.. hoo hoo.."

Catatonic cause and effects war cool about nothing because I couldn't tell where the music was coming from.. Mass-itches.. I was compelled how the front door drops bass like cotton swabs and the back door breaks a broken house throbbing in the fall of the trouble for her holy hall-o-Kaws'd...

The hiss'd dick tendency test zone is about self control altruism.. attempting self control abductionx.. Fee-illing and key-illing in order to create program daws for planting dings on them..

So many of the others are daw's bowl backed for sexual insinuations that does or would not have a clause of competence.. The school rules is because he doesn't.. and or they don't .. whoever the fuck they are.. And the people are the salt of the public as is only a concept of the surgery step..

Fed-her-hall-he-clause'd - you have to have complete control over me or I'm not going to do the right thing? He gets lust or he leaves.. trying to have control over her is not hiss? house..

How to file a warrant regarding sexual insinuations was not in the DARE camp.. Checking into the jail and filing a retort or a violation.. was not in DARE camp ... But they did tell the US to use a condom.. in DARE camp.. for trafficking drugs?

"it" chose fucking? I would need to check into jail and file a warrant in my own words..

Because she hiss-tailing about.. he can't read and write.. and speaking to an officer is a scapegoat of discretion.. The cop is a daw.. you can't read and write as the officer insists.. And people don't to need to understand what they accuse eachother of?

the practice insists as a form of a question in a transforming perception..

act shunz war haw'r-daw'r than words ..He doesn't know what it's worth and he's the words .. fuck him.. for hymn.. the practice of anti-intelligence and non-human sacrifice about the "lord.. ho-sis" as the cops practice the HI-SIS.. I found my reflection at the leg..lake.. and the closet personality told me to take a bath in sugar and eat the salt? They yell about in anger and what it sounded like in tungs is .. that's the rounds.. Running owe'd of water.. and you need to pooosh some blood back to that error yea..

Sex prooved he wasn't scared but its a foul against hymn.. because he can't prove that.. Smoking may or can and or.. will stop bad oweez.. hypnosis'.. that you needed to earn the right to be able to physically fight or hit other people.. B-kaws people who don't know.. are promotive of self destructive and or accident prone.. So look at that car-sin-again.. well guess what.. we aren't allowed to be homeless and poor..its illegal and I am .. su-us-idle..

so I was just.. trying to say that.. being poor and homeless is illegal.. If I didn't have to spend time in prison to say that.. I must've been lucky? Mating information schemes that are intended to have anti house concepts.. And animal atraxtion methods of retrieval beta trend as she thinks he sounds like.. he's just ouw'd of it as the bars close and the invisible door slams..

The bot-he's bitter .. check my pulse and tell me if you can hear a catastrofree.. I was abducted by a sexy-wall as an edible.. blueberries made her into .. a missed hit.. sheeeesh adversity.. it just own's me .. demon shunned even as a poly-cotton blend..

And well hell.. it needs to know ..so that the genomes can decide..

I think my body forgot what bear foot feels like.. When the kleptomania costs me impulse control and or compulsive disorderly conduct made from a born to steal and fart like glorious blasphemy.. Telepathy simulations further and farther.. and better paying for telepathy abilities is so.. ow'ed of it.. And minimal terrorism stole the good times from under my bed.. On a more uber perspective I had to think that I'm just shit floating in the pond..

The truck fight

"I think I noticed them smoking US on empty.. I know that would.. punch all the safety switches on.."

Brian thinks out loud rubbing some road dust from his face and wishing that he could find another truck wash for his dogmatism.. Sitting up as the warmth of the sun had splashed onto him from across the rows of dirt filling an empty farmland feeling of hot air..

"I must've been so high last night.." -Potatoman

"How.. stoned.. does it get?" -Brian asks

"At this point it doesn't matter.. Talking about last night will only get me lost.. is like fools gold, and the end of all the tricks stand like water on the brain.. but that nothing was ..only the smoke.. that smoke was the water too.." -Potatoman

"Yo man.. life is not a beer fight in the mailroom building cracks like soggy dreams.." -Brian

The potato-man kicks some sand and dust whirlwinding a rock and skipping it like a whip across the pavement's crunchy crackles..

"I know I know.. I think I'll have to change my schedule to one week on.. and one week off.." -Potatoman

"They need you but they don't.. 1.. 2.." -Brian murmurs as he jumps up and smacks his legs and arms from the still of sleep that may have been containing the time he doesn't want to waist..

As time being the gods on wheels that owned the shades under the trees.. Concepts of inducing intercoarse with the spirit of god by using an individual of who.. Happens as social home-lock as a case.. under the pay-rental scheme .. she thinks as is.. touching myself could.. be "inhumane" ruled with weed and tobacco compared together.. against the water on the brain concept..

He's the sugar and she's the salt is what.. was the lead suspect to the fame as the tea party creates a new flavor of coffee boiled from the machine head of muse..

I suspect the iDEA is paying the people to chase the time into really stupidly complicated financial problems'.. As anti-mortalism.. Enforcing the fouls of moral propositions.. She teaches a hard lesson about change .. Don't follow vague clues with desperate poor people that have no life to change to begin with.. the other part of the lesson is.. 90 percent of society would be able to fit in the poor people category ..but 90 percent of them will deny that they are homeless and insist that they aren't poor people.. So then you surpassed 90 percent ..but then you lost the power in numbers equation..

Less is more has a draw of interest but it's too vague.. your a sex crazed lost puppy that gets addicted to drugs or your queer.. Concentrates and Contra-inceptives into sub-rooted rule breaker fetish.. breaking rules in ways that people don't notice as a covert'd offensive tact.. towards the character as animal abduction .. psychological yoga manifestations' makes minimal terrorism a Nationwide standard..

So what's the magic question?

What would cause paranoia is just magic awareness'.. And Who's asking as the answere'd?

But I found that the secret is that ..it should kill you if you fast on alcohol.. you don't notice it's going to kill you if you are hyped on at least a little bit of cocaine or meth.. but lucky for the hero.. drunk people bleed out faster..

Just as a reflex ..is explainable.. as moral compass.. only a really intellectual dude really knows and hates how dumb it is.. and how dumb she is.. and how dumb they are..

following hymn with the antics to hurt your apatight.. or ruin it..

I don't know why we can't just sit down and calm down..

Must be some bullshit about native americans conceptualized like a double negative stereo.. Radio-ing release of responsibility combined as a guilt trap about being white..

Most likely.. another style of intentionally forgotten.. Exampled.. as a paranoya you can never identify with.. And the body bag was bugged.. driving the incentive but the blood lets ..like salt melts..

Society advanced into an intermediate qweer using the chicken wire to trap hymn.. They made the plague and they planted it in empty shelter places.. for nobody to find..

And Ray Charles wasn't really blind..

And they who.. have eyes that work?

ultra-moral capa-city excites paranoia ratios' ..until the salt is the water and the sugar is the weed..

Purple haze'd all through my wifi signal.. And claimed alcohol was much more honest.. Based about how the invention of too much.. made her sick..

And if you paid for a service.. paying money is what makes it water.. or maybe.. it was the weed..

..so smoke is water and water is smoke ..and if you know what that would mean.. then you graduated as an illuminescent'd kidney stone survivor.. Surgeon General Warning .. coffee is very high in phosphorus..

We would suggest against drinking coffee on an empty stomach..

And so.. these algebra's ..is what it's from.. Brian thought to himself as he squinted far ahead through all the offspring of the bad religion.. An off-ramp ahead wrecked like grilled grease and it must be the onions is what Brian thought as the salvation curled every taste bud.. The traffic stops are rich in drive through service that becomes the bedrock for the wanderer on the crossroad of falling off of it.. Like an air pushing pirate that never sailed.. We got beef ora.. Eeeek-walls the square'd root of fast food.. For this hero .. Begging for a cheeseburger was outside of the box.. because asking for change was also a bit too much..

"Hi, never learned to hunt ..can you help me out?" Brian imagined he would have to continue asking for longer than a minute.. But the very first person he asked was happy to buy hymn a sandwich.. Actually 2 sandwiches.. "And that was the interesting advantage of the power of the cheeseburger chump.." -Brian chomps away as he crumples one of the cheeseburger wrappers and shoots the paper-foil ball into a garbage can..

"And with a mouth full of algebra that stifled the stamina of common resources.." -the potato man claimed..

"And I promise that I will never kiss my mother.." -Brain laughs.. with a chomp full and such..

"You better go back for a milkshake.." -the potato man suggests..

"Hey man .. I can tie my own shoes.." -Brain blurts as a half a burp.. - "Besides .. I got a free soda.. out of the deal.."

"Ha.. hawww.." -laughs the potato man.. "So, that's how free works?"

Brain almost chokes but laughs it off and continues with the last munch of the second burger..

"Well I know you never tied your shoe with one hand.. could a fair shake ever happen with one hand?" -Brian

"And so that question is just that ..what algebra is from?" -The potato man segregates the question as imperfection can be..

"Well, what do you think we really ate as un-evolved? Bread was the social evolution.. Right? Obviously.. Hunting wasn't an advantage for city born people.." -Brian insists as the last chomping of the burgers salutates..

Social patterns and implying them to see the future is rationably a multiplied incentive of reflection of those blues.. Such warrants are part of the rainbow ..but the sky was divided by them baby blues.. Some people like bluegrass ..but plants can't be blue.. You need an architect to connect those dots and let the idea live.. in ancient arabic the sky was considered green.. And the green grew.. As the green was blue and the blue wasn't even noticed .. That algebraic social whatevers'.. of some considerations about the cup being full or empty.. I could agree that it ..was a passive aggressive offense.. And chimpanzees have better long term memory because they can't talk? Yeah, like we must be.. less bedder because we can talk..

And that might explain dis-leg-see-yea.. like moral licensing..

..dead headz can't hang in the lust of reality as it squeezes ..

..but I think I was trying to prove that I wasn't lost in the innuendo..

..God could make hymn lost.. but she wasn't.. without hymn..

As Brian looked up and focussed more.. the afternoon slaggering past over a couple of hours of riding.. it had seemed only about a day from the last camp out.. That he had found a water tap.. And smudging the mustard and tomato from his loins .. With the perfect flavor of mystery tap.. Mostly carelessness is ok for the hero of the wanderers.. In a sick forgetful way..

And as Brian becomes of himself upon another sting of miles like a flying tip toe contest.. Maybe he snuck up to the buildings closest to the Casino and Cards.. A bar and a night club about as shiny as black powder.. The pool was inside.. so Brian had to skip a rinse..

"The future has high security.." -potato man creeps

"Yeah.. And a real strip bar.." -Brian says back and walking back across the parking lot with the water bottles filled.. The old 10 speed was already handle barred into a fence as Brian stopped and sat.. to think.. As some shade was moving across the parking areas he sat and watched the supposed people of status as if.. And he guessed and gathered about what he thought that they would think.. But the few hours left tempered quickly as the Sun's glare was eventually dimmed and Brian laid against the brick building across the lot as the heat continued to radiate after the breeze had cooled.. those contrasts of yellow and red mixing at the end of a day can feel like it was the right place and the right time..

"HEy, you.." -A voice drummed around until he realized he was waking up again.. And then as Brian came to the surface of his eyelids .. He opened his eyes, still half leaning against the warm bricks like a sick puppy that he was..

"Are you ok?" -Hot chick..

"Holy.. holy holy.." -Brian couldn't believe his eyes as the smell of oils and perfume that caused more blood to slam into his head.. "No.. not that one.. the other one.." -Brian murmured as he woke up blurred into the view of a twenty something year old beautiful hottie.. slendered against the butch of the block..

"What are you doing here.. Are you drunk?" -the hot chick asked

"What? Do I smell drunk?" -says Brian as he yawns all huge.. "I think and I'm just tired.."

"Well, somebody might see you out here.. but you don't have a car." SHe thinks.. "I thought you were a dead person.. this isn't a safe area.. You could get beat up or something.."

"What? ..this is better than dead.. Who's gunna beat me up?"
-Brian picks his head up and looking around and such..

"So.. OK.. it's still early.. but there will be more people.. in a couple of hours.. And I have seen dead people out here before.."
-The hottie chick says

Brian slags over into .. rolling across the concrete some couple of feet and gasping and sounding like a soul that could consider giving up on nothing.. "I'm so dirty from this dirty ass life and this stupid bike.."

"The hot chick looked around and noticed the bike.. "So that is how you got here.. that bike? You look like a highschool kid.. How old are you?"

"I'm 19.." -Brian sherks up and sits up.. with his shirt off and stunted like a sweaty youngster.. "I'm not dead.." -Brian says.. "I'm just thinking.. but maybe I'm a lost puppy ..just like the story says.."

"Like, the story says?" The hot chick in black tight pants and a casino staff shirt turns and looks across the par-keying lot..

"I just wish I had a magic bathroom button or something.." -Brain kackles.. He reaches to grab his hoodie while rolling over into the warm wall again and wraps it around his head moaning in a weird tired'd way..

"A magic bathroom button? Where the hell did you come from? I've never seen anybody on a bike riding through here.. Do you even know where the hell you are?" The young hottie asks

"How did I get here? Why would I get beat up? Are you going to get beat up?" -Brian asks

"No.. I wouldn't get beat up.. but you might if you stay here for the evening.. The dudes that come around here are dumbasses'.." -she says

"Wow.. what a cool job.. must be nice being a hot chick working as a gamble ..and you don't have to care about society.."

-Brain responds like a fish out of water.. blubbering on nothing.. "Must be so fancy having a Vagina.."

The hot chick laughs.. and stoops down to crutch against the curb.. "oh ok.. I think you're funny or something.. um.. Maybe I have.. or something like.." -she seems to space off..

"Maybe you have.. what?" -Brian asks as he swoops his hoodie over his top half.. And the breeze seemed to bluff and fluff suddenly as the hot chick thought about it..

"I could get you a bath but you have to promise that you will never come back here ever again.." -hottie

"You could?" -Brian asks with interest..

"These are all private properties'.. around here.. I have actually seen people get killed around here.." -hot chick

"Yeah.. private.. ok .. What the hell does any of that have to do with me? I'm not a missing person.. and besides I know that's just a thing that people say to people like me.." -Brian

"Whatever then ..Nevermind .. Just follow me.. if you want a bath so bad.." - hot chick leads ..

"Just follow you? Should I bring the bike?" -Brian

"Quit fucking around .. Do you want a bath or not?" -hot chick

Brian grabs up his backpack and the bike from its handle-barred stunt.. The hot chick struts towards a fenced area that had been cut open and the chain link fence was rolled to the side with an opening big enough to walk through.. it fits ..only one person at a time.. Brian followed the hot chick about some unpaved streets and simple homes planted in a situation of a small village like .. trailer homes but no trailers..

A street path on the farther side of the small block was especially quiet..

"OK.. so it's monday.. there would be people around here on most of the week.. but not mondays and tuesdays.. So.. it should be .. nobodies there.." - She swerves and points to a faded looking house that might have been a blue color at another time..

"This is a bath-house?" -Brian asks

Yeah, well that's what this street is for.. all these houses on this street are bath houses.."

"What about the other houses?" -Brian

"Don't ask.. and don't mess around.." - She says as she walks off.. and struts like a whip.. back to the fence-line .. and then shouts .. "You're not my problem.. people do.. get hurt around here.."

Brain steps up to the door and notices the older style handle was busted and as if ..the door was busted into at some point or another.. And that wasn't any problem for Brian as he noticed the door still had another latch and pin as he pushed the door open with his foot.. He could smell fruity soap smells like the aroma of a spa and so.. The front room of the house was filled with piles of vhs movies that formed a city of vhs piled over everything in the room and entryway.. maybe there was a table under there somewhere.. but whatever it was.. It was completely owned by the cities of VHS.. A huge 50 inch screen stood tall facing the front window as if ..perfect viewing from the porch.. A standard of several types of VHS players stacked around a mess of wires that may have been plugged together since the time that land forgot was remembered.. Also many more electronical dings that seemed to flutter the entryway closet.. But there he was.. in the backside of a who knows what.. jocking a shower from the casino's dis-leg-see-ya candidate.. And he found the bathroom racked with oils and bath salts.. And as his social stagnations' in full blown fail'd.. Brian lavished in the hot crunch of nowhere.. And as if sexy was nerdy or nerdy was salty.. social stamina skills are relaxed and refreshed as if to stifle the purple from the blood of the lamb.. And as exhausting as all that seems to feel.. He had these thoughts ..And that maybe.. he thought.. he wasn't feeling it.. as he fell asleep in the tub..

Loud clunks and pops slam on a frequent sense of nerve wrecked.. After lights out.. the sounds of the bays and the cell door systems shutting down is a comfort in the symbol of complexion.. We don't know why or how it works is that.. Faith-Fuck in effect.. And that Bay lock down sequence begins like clockwork for the timing of intermediate safe-tease mode that isn't supposed to make you hurt yourself and or others.. Some doors clank and clunk as the guards continue to rotate the hourly walk through procedures.. Perhaps, it was unaccountable as the lordosis is war-keying as a defective social accountability status.. Scoliosis might have been the evidence of how it went too far.. But they war just making sure that I was getting twisted up.. The guard enters the cell bay as the lights are down.. A young female in her twenties.. A young man that waits for court stands in the window of the cell door waiting to see her as a visual stump of authority.. Humor as Torcher..

"Isn't it past.. your a bedtime.." - She stands vexingly and greets the young male in question..

The youngster requested.. that he had been asking for a paper and pencil since a couple days ago.. But the day shift guards had been forgetting to get him a pencil and paper.. Maybe, it was a monday on repeat.. as my dream seduced me .. as the victim of loss cause..

The young guard on the night shift reaches into her breast pocket and passes a pencil under the door..

The Truck Fight

Knocking sounds as an echoing of repetitiveness as Brian realizes he's been woken up again by the sounds of the night shift guards doing the walk through shift checks.. He gets up to look out the cell window..

The female guard is on night shift again.. She must have thought that I had to go non-house.. because I thought I didn't need to beat anybody.. in school.. and I couldn't prove something.. about how or if I had fear or not.. as I attended to the good grades and spitting was a sensitive subject..

"Mr. Loose.. isn't it.. pissed ..your a bedtime?" -She ask'd..

I would guess that.. blood as nothing was the extremely kweer blooper that incited alcohol at the gas stations.. as if it was water.. And it still is extremely kweer..

Brian woke up dazed and soaked to the bone..

"And the salt helped and.. maybe it was worth it.." -Brian thought muttering.. just lightly enough for himself to hear.. He slowly decided to climb out of the tub before it gets weird.. Then he suddenly realized why he woke up.. Some sounds .. from the entry rooms ..and the door being opened and shut a couple of times and ..

Brian sits on the bathroom floor waiting to dry and slowly he sets his backpack between his legs and just about the same moment as he slowly puts his hoodie on.. he can hear the kitchen sink and some objects being tossed around.. Her voice sounds dry and cracked and she then cries a little bit.. Brian sits listening and trying to guess what the situation could be and suddenly .. He hears her drunkenly scream as she starts bantering about something.. then dialing a phone number.. The bathroom door is cracked open and Brian can smell booze in the air.. He sits still and considering to jump up and just leave.. but he was so soaked.. Momentarily he checks in his bag for the small pistol that he had found..

The clip was full of rounds and he had checked it before.. A crumpled stomp and then rushed footsteps sounding like a stumbling idiot.. The door jammed open and she stumbled and stopped suddenly..

"Who the fuck?" -she says "You aren't.. What the hell are you doing here?"

Brian sat thinking for a moment as he saw smoke from her ciggerrette brush into her eyes.. as she then whipped the glass from her hand and it smashes somewhere behind him.. And it was an odd moment for him.. As a non-focussed squeeze ..Brian had shot the gun at that moment of such a case that the event.. Even he wasn't sure if he had done it himself.. Such a slow moment .. She fell and her head bounced off the floor a couple of times.. making it all more real.. He looked down as gunsmoke rolled from the inside of his back-pack.. In a state of unbelief that the one shot could kill her.. Blood began spreading across the floor and Brian jumped up and grabbed his jeans and started putting them on.. Feelings of adrenaline mixed with a blank of the thought that.. he may have just killed somebody.. Brian dry-heaved a couple of times just before puking on her.. Still with only one leg in his pants.. And trying not to lose his balance and fall on her.. He then both legged his pants into one of the silliest awkward bounces over a dead drunk girl and out of the house.. By the time he made it to the highway he realized he had left the bike and he wasn't going back for it..

It could've been about 3:30 AM or so.. Walking along the highway.. West as it goes..

"My family liked to argue, but not for the right reasons.." -The potato man's voice sustained as Brian's ears war still ringing..

"At least you knew that.." -Brian says

"I think I didn't know what kind of humor I was observing.." -Potatoman says

"I started lying young.. When I was 9.. I thought it was funny to tell my mom that I forgot what time it was.. I think didn't do it on purpose though.. Do you believe that?" -Brian asks

"That's a darker side of sarcastic ..like after it built a wall and burned it down.." - potatoman

"I think all females should be considered as interns.." -Brian

The potatoman differentiates- "Well don't tell me that .. nobody assumes that all women are attracted to getting money for sex.."

"And there are so many views through the water.. and how to hold it.." -Brian thinks'..

"But getting loud and making money without hurting anybody would be a control point escape.." -Potatoman shreeks

"Maybe it's just that she devoured a high dive of love over intuition.. like a control-alt-delete.. knowing why becomes a psychological yoga map about a parallel intention.." -Brian elaborates "Money was cool because then the art would.. And he could prove how she lied about sex.. This is what.. the courthouse people keep mindfucking the men of private business.. about the meeting.. She thinks it's empty but he wants it.. 2 be full.. SHE is the EMT and he had to be a fool.. as a far fetch that never bites back.. and only can come back.. or disappear making hymn a fancy health problems' without touching you.. The counterfeit karma is preprogrammed as a fancy interjection.. of fait-fucked as inner-jack-shunz.. but those nobodies are left out and their unfortunate life is a living memory as a burn in the court.. Room to remember that it happens.. like the first time .. again and again.. because the public is lost.. as an unfortunate whim of excuses.. to abuse.. and get lost over and over.. Healing as bad news.. The House isn't broken.. but it is ..for hymn.. mr. public.. loves hiss .. shoes.. they told hymns.. You can't live.. outside.. as that "cold space experiment" ..But they can't remember where he is supposed to go..

The potato man retorts as a medium of social insight.. "Ya know, squatting hasn't been real since 1885.. especially for boys that don't have a woman with kids.."

"Yeah.. I think I noticed.. that.." -Brian slanders with ease..

A couple of cars had passed by but Brian hadn't even waved and he reached into his bag and sparked a cigarette.. And then it must've been that .. Perhaps the glow from the cigarette as a car that was hot rodding passed Brian heading west decided to stop and help somebody with a ride..

The car reved up after swerving and screeching to a stop.. Whomping and burning rubber in reverse as Brian jumps off the concrete into the grass.. The hot rodded old mustang was faded perl and primer.. All original chrome and the glass was clean.. Brain decided to get in without much consideration as his adrenaline was on high and his temper was glory holed in the most respectful dissent.. Getting off of the highway and far from where he was became the motivation of careless love.. The jackass driving said he was driving west and that's all he ask'd.. But .. Sometimes things just happen all the wrong way.. For a reason.. After the dude popped a beer and offered Brian one.. Brian took the beer and put it in his back pack and sat waiting .. And finishing his cigarette..

"I'm not in the mood.. I'll save it for later.. " -Brian says

"So what the hell happened? You wouldn't happen to have any glass?" The dude asks..

"Glass?" -Brian asks strange'd

"You know.. Some powder?" -The dude asks

"Man, I don't know anything about that.. I just want to see the Ocean.." -Brian says

"Well you got a long fucking way to go bro.. thats hella far from where I'm going.." -The dude swerves and reaches for something or another like how a tweaker drives on crack..

"Yeah.. You ever been to the Ocean?" -Brian asks as an attempt to reflect with the drunk person or ..

"HA hA.. That's fucking hilarious that you ask .. Because I thought I was in the ocean maaan!" - the dude whomps on the gas and starts driving like a jackass that Brian was realizing he was.. The horse power hugged the road and the vehicle was really throttled the heavier way..

Brian grabbed the seat and held his backpack next to the door..

"Holy Shit .. Sounds impressive.. man .. I think.. I want to live through this though.." -Brian says as he braces his left hand up to the dashboard..

"I drive everyday and.. I ain't never wrecked.. yet.." -the dude laughs as he starts chugging the beer he just popped open in his hand..

Brian stalls in the moment as the view of the glee of nature suspended in his perspectives .. also considering that the jerk behind the wheel could be normal.. And then Brian is looking away.. out the window as he can see the potato man on the side of the highway with a large sign.. And Brian could see the sign said..

BLOOD or WATER with a huge question mark..

This slow motion mind fart boosted Brian into a bitterland mode of adrenaline and mixed with a fortune rich of culture shock.. Brian started laughing really hard and then with one hand on the handle of the door.. He boosted the drunk driving dude in the face.. Kicking hard kicks as the car swerved.. Brian leaned against the inside of the door as the old vinyl crunched and the car seemed to moan in the moment as the car began to flip and just as the car flipped .. Brian jammed on the handle and the door flipped with the momentum of the car flipping and Brian was flung from the car.. as a spinning object from the vehicle.. And some people believe that circus tricks are things that are practiced over and over.. Brian found himself still alive and when he staggered to get up.. His leg seemed to have hit the big one.. Limping over to the car after it flipped into the disaster Brian dreamed about.. The drunk driver was bled out ..almost.. Brian pulled the small handgun out of the backpack and shot the dude once in his head..

Still getting a breath.. Brian stands there staring at the scene a moment.. He slags the gun back into the backpack and considering the differences of careless love and how those ends meet.. He cracked open the beer and poured it all out on the fine equation.. And he kept walking..

It's anybody's guess about .. what time it was..

Burned by this noooo... Thing.. As a mutual progress in mutual progress' of the social enterprise reeling wishes that promise stigma like a pair of loaded dice.. Thinking that predetermined falicy.. as if it was hymn at fault like a broken record..

Walking happens for those who wait among the fishery men lures.. And the musicians' of hymn are that city-scum that scrub the barrels for the grooves.. And the scene stirs like a personality trainwreck having a birthday party for moral aptitude.. And staying still by avoiding conflict as that LOVE species.. Finding Power in nothing is also nothing to know about. Because you don't know how to make them work.. Depending on whether or not you choose to put poop in mailboxes or or break windows like a software testing.. Keeping track of the credit system Rocked my brains into peaces of shit flying like they say.. As if I could change time and space while defining the coincidences' to the public at large as happenstance? I would have to study addiction and motor sensory as innate fear and undermine the purpose of the sixth senses as an excuse to hack the self composition of stupid.. I know I get it because I know Im stupid as "it" can get..

It's like an ugly reflection in the morning that makes you feel cute but most people don't see it because they suck at accentuating.. And so the innate connected sixth senses are perhaps assumed to be transformable by remote causes and such confusion is stupid excelling as a shining beacon of what we believed .. Give thanks for right or wrong that never asks for anything in return.. And if you could prove that pissing could be a clown based talent then stupid will or should excell for a million self explained blunders.. Perhaps you might get a better reflection of your hands.. And perhaps you could act as if it mattered so that the innuendo could predict and or even cause a trapezoidal episode.. Brian would suggest that you build some momentum by remembering the first time you felt stupid like your life depends on it.. Assuming that as an individual nobody you can't actually explain what the money market does on a world scale.. Because if you could explain it.. You would be double crossing what the bible DARE's to protect..

Prelude

This hopeless novel example of hindsight was brought to ..US.. as attention..

A war-kneeing statement crafted as the sick sensibility we argue if we need or want.. Assuming that conversation is as valuable as understanding the Dejavudoo of our brains on drugs.. The program asses-mentalism of the contraceptives that blindside like night vision.. Code chains that root from the dirty-bak-rub stem avid causes .. Some report lucid moral atrophy.. Others argued whether or not sex trafficking was a sport or a form of torture as the memory banks beefed up.. Choosy cross training leads many others into the Honey crutch system as the heart rocks cultures.. The tragedy case catastrophe stalled like it was programmed to do.. but the studs didn't worry because they had trouble coded insurance policies.. The charge officials thought talking was swinging as a lust competition antic and most suckers think Ha-key is a bit too much.. As an author of national security sequences.. Some tragedy cases contacted the psychic hotlines as alternative measures of powerlifting to build control points.. Condescending reflexes became arguable in many cases of underdog strategy as the excuses to survive may or may not be about avoiding blue-balls.. They might suggest chewing on salt and see if that helps..

I wished that I was anywhere but here
I couldn't believe my eyes
I wanted to escape and walk away
Some things are hard for sight
But I know I need to think about it
And it seems that is the way they found it
A story very hard to find
A serious question about the truth
Did I ever tell you what they know?
The story of the black and blue
Shoe sonny shoe sonny shoe
Don't take me for know fool
I didn't get here pinchin pennies
Boy they could care less about you too
Better know right now you'll never crow this loud
Even the roosters gotta pay his dues
Is it the American dream?
Well don't be thinkin that you do
They thought that she could have the world by sell'n it to you
I don't know why you have to learn it all the hard way
No heart No soul No shirt No shoes
No service for this tool
Did I ever tell you about what they know
A serious question about the truth
The story of the Black and Blue
You think your smart sonny

Then they don't care
You're too smart buddy
Have a drink or two
Better walk away cause can't you see they don't play
Shoe sonny shoe sonny shoe
A serious question about the truth
They really like her but they really don't like you
I don't know why you gotta learn it all the hard way
She smiles through a bad attitude
Dr. Uncle's your brother and all fizzin full of booze
And they want you to think that too
Just don't spook the hor says
You got nothin and thats the way it will stay
Somethin for nothin anyway
They got nothin
They want to proove
I don't know why you gotta learn it all the hard way

This book is in thoughts of those who have served by fire-fight with our Armed Forces and also in reconsideration for cases of social unrest that include violent protest.. Rethink... Drive intuit..

www.ingramcontent.com/pod-product-compliance
Lightning Source LLC
Chambersburg PA
CBHW050420110726
47899CB00008B/2781